Many of Cather   –
but perhaps that   or
is herself a bit o   –
Martin Waddell   ks
as the Little Dracula series, *Little Obie and the Flood*
and *Can't You Sleep, Little Bear?* (winner of the
Smarties Book Prize and Kate Greenaway Medal).

So why the two names? "I use the name Catherine
Sefton for longer, more emotionally based books,"
the author explains, "while most of my Martin
Waddell titles are simply fun. Sefton is a family name
and Catherine is a clear bright name – and I wanted
my books to have a clear bright feeling about them."
Another feature of the Sefton books is their Irish
backgrounds. Ballaghbeg, for example, the setting
for *The Back House Ghosts*, is modelled on
Newcastle, County Down, where the author has
lived for the past twenty years. His house at the foot
of the Mountains of Mourne bears a close resem-
blance to the Bon Vista guest house, the home of the
book's heroine Ellen and her family.

Catherine Sefton's many titles include *In a Blue
Velvet Dress* (Walker Books, 1991) and *Starry Night*
which won the Other Award.

Also by Catherine Sefton

The Blue Misty Monsters
Emer's Ghost
The Emma Dilemma
The Ghost Girl
In a Blue Velvet Dress
Island of the Strangers
Shadows on the Lake
The Sleepers on the Hill

By Martin Waddell

Fred the Angel
Little Obie and the Flood
Little Obie and the Kidnap
Our Sleepysaurus

THE
BACK HOUSE GHOSTS

Catherine Sefton

WALKER BOOKS
LONDON

First published 1974 by Faber and Faber Limited
This edition published 1991 by Walker Books Ltd
87 Vauxhall Walk, London SE11 5HJ

Reprinted 1991

© 1974 Catherine Sefton
Cover illustration © 1991 Anne Yvonne Gilbert

Printed and bound in Great Britain by
Cox and Wyman Ltd, Reading, Berkshire

British Library Cataloguing in Publication Data
Sefton, Catherine
The back house ghosts.
I. Title
823'.914 [F]
ISBN 0-7445-2057-6

O come to me, beloved,
And stay here, by my side.
O come to me, beloved,
At the turning of the tide.

I'll come to you, beloved,
I'll stay by your side.
I'll come to you, beloved,
At the turning of the tide.

CHAPTER 1

"Eleven!" exclaimed Mrs Bailey.

"Eleven children," said Bella. "If you count Mr and Mrs Mooney as well, there are thirteen of them, and we've got two doubles and a single to put them in."

"You've excelled yourself this time, Ellen!" groaned Mrs Bailey.

"It would be Ellen!" said Bella accusingly.

Ellen sat at the kitchen table, feeling foolish. "I'm just disaster-prone, I suppose," she said.

Even for Ellen it was a major mistake. As a result of it, eleven Mooneys plus their father and mother were fretting in the front room of Bon Vista, waiting to be shown to their rooms.

If Ellen was annoyed about it, so was Mrs Mooney.

First of all she removed the baby Mooney from her husband's arms, deftly inserted its bottle between its lips, and handed it over to the nearest medium-sized Mooney. Then she cornered Mr Mooney by the window.

"I don't think that that girl in the Tourist Caravan can have explained about us properly," she said. "Did you notice the landlady's face when we came in?"

Mr Mooney had noticed it. He could hardly miss it.

When Mrs Bailey opened the front door, her face was wreathed in welcoming smiles. "So nice to see you," she beamed. "Did you have a ... pleasant ... journ ... oh!"

One Mooney after another came into the hall, and at least two of them were clad only in pyjamas.

"Are these all ... oh, dear!" Mrs Bailey's question wavered away into a mumble.

"Ours?" said Mrs Mooney. "Didn't they tell you?"

Ellen had taken the phone call from the Tourist Caravan. It was a very bad line, and every time the girl at the other end spoke, there was a crackle. Ellen had managed to make out what she thought were the important bits. Yes, they had vacancies. Yes, they could manage full board. Special terms would *depend*.

"Crackle crackle crackle family?" asked the phone.

"What?"

"Crackle mind crackle children?"

8

"Sorry, could you say that again? This line is awful."

"Yes, crackle it? Crackle crackle crackle baby?"

"What do they want?" Mrs Bailey called from the landing. The sound of the telephone had brought her dripping from the bath, draped in a large towel, with a pink plastic bag on her head. She had plucked up the courage to give herself a blue rinse, and the phone call had come in the nick of time. Now, as she stood shivering on the landing, she was having second thoughts.

Ellen put her hand over the receiver. "I think they're asking if we can take a family for a fortnight. Can we?"

"How many?" asked Mrs Bailey, as the puddle round her feet spread across the landing carpet.

Ellen relayed the question.

"*Well*," said the phone, cautiously, "crackle crackle eleven crackle crackle baby. Crackle crackle small, though. Is that crackle right?"

"What do they say?" said Mrs Bailey impatiently.

"I think they're asking if we can take a child of eleven and a small baby, plus mother and father," said Ellen.

"Of course," said Mrs Bailey.

"Yes, we can manage that easily," Ellen reported back.

"Crackle crackle crackle magnificent!" said the voice at the other end, sounding both relieved and surprised. "Do crackle crackle favour sometime, too, crackle crackle. Crackle you crackle much indeed!"

High tea for the residents was due at 5.30. At half-past four the new arrivals appeared, all thirteen of them. They were cross, for someone had stolen their minibus in the first week of a three-week holiday. With it had gone some of their money and most of their clothes.

"I wonder how those two got caught in their pyjamas?" Ellen muttered, but no one paid any attention to her.

"Consider yourself an untouchable," said Bella, who was two years older than Ellen.

"I didn't do it deliberately," protested Ellen.

"We can't manage it," said Mrs Bailey. "We haven't got enough room. I shall have to tell them so."

She went out to speak to Mr and Mrs Mooney.

"Oh dear," said Mr Mooney.

"I just don't know where to turn," said a weary Mrs Mooney. "And the children will be so disappointed!"

"It's all my fault!" said Ellen, who was listening at the kitchen door.

"Don't stand there moaning about it," said Bella. "Ring Mrs Stewart, see if she can take

10

some of them." Ellen rang Mrs Stewart. She also rang Sea Breezes, Fairmount, Cliff House, Dun-Roamin', and Balthazar, but it was the week of the Fireworks Display, and no one had any room.

"Now I know why that girl from the Tourist Caravan sounded so relieved!" said Ellen.

Mrs Bailey came back into the kitchen. "Ellen," she said. "I wonder if Mrs Stewart might be…"

Ellen shook her head. "I've rung them all," she said.

"That poor woman, with all those children, having to traipse back to Belfast and no holiday!"

Silence fell in the kitchen.

At the same moment silence had fallen in the dining-room, as the junior Mooneys were informed that their only-just-begun holiday was over.

"I know!" exclaimed Bella. "The back house!"

Mrs Bailey had looked up hopefully when she heard her daughter's exclamation, but now she shook her head. "We couldn't put people in there," she said. "It's damp, and you can see through the roof because it has lost so many slates. Even if it was in reasonable order we haven't got any furniture for it. I doubt if anyone has lived there for years."

11

Ellen looked at Bella.

Bella looked at Ellen.

"It isn't as bad as all that," Ellen said.

"Not all of it," said Bella.

"What do you mean?" asked Mrs Bailey.

"We tidied it up," said Ellen. "We had to have somewhere to retreat to in the summer when there were guests all over the place, and we couldn't sit down in our own house. You don't mind, do you?"

"We didn't spend any money," said Bella quickly. "We just patched up the roof with old felt from the shed, and tidied up inside."

"Mind?" said Mrs Bailey. "Of course I don't mind. But I don't think we could put guests in there."

"Not guests," said Bella. "Us!"

"Oh," said Mrs Bailey.

"We could take down those old iron bedsteads from the loft," said Ellen. "If we put them in the back house we could sleep there, and do the cooking and everything else in here … so long as it doesn't rain!"

Mrs Bailey made a face. "I'm a bit old for camping out," she said.

Next door one of the smaller Mooneys began to cry.

"It was my fault," said Ellen. "I'd like to do something to put it right."

"I don't..." Mrs Bailey began, but she looked at Ellen's face, and changed her mind. "Let's have a look at the house, anyway," she said. "I suppose it might be possible."

The house was at the end of the garden, against the Demesne wall. It had lime-washed walls and four tiny windows, just big enough to take a head and shoulders. They had straightened the horseshoe on the front door, and trimmed the rambling rose that ran up the rusted gutter-pipe and across one of the windows. In the downstairs window Ellen had placed a rose in a milk-bottle.

Ellen pushed the half-door open and they ducked their heads to pass through the low doorway.

"This must have been the living-room," said Ellen. "And the fireplace has an arm for a pot, and a pair of old bellows." A flight of narrow stairs ran up the side wall, and Ellen led the way up. A clock with no minute hand hung on the landing. "No works either!" said Bella. Two doors opened off the landing, one to each of two tiny rooms.

"It's small," said Ellen. "But it must have been very cosy and warm in winter with those big thick walls."

"Made of boulders from the beach, and mud and clay all mixed up," said Bella. "I suppose that that is why it is all crooked!"

"I suppose it is safe?" said Mrs Bailey, as the floorboards creaked beneath her feet. She put her hand on the mantelpiece, and it came away dusty. "If you call this clean, I don't think much of your housekeeping!"

"We haven't had much time recently," said Ellen.

That was true.

The Baileys had to work hard all summer, cooking breakfasts and making beds and stopping the guests doing silly things, like bathing in strong currents or taking three-year-olds on hikes up the Black Mountain. "Fool board", Bella called it, rather unkindly, but everyone knew what she meant. While their schoolfriends went off on holiday to Spain and Italy and other places, the Baileys stayed at home in Ballaghbeg helping their mother to run Bon Vista, because the money they earned in the summer had to keep them through the winter.

"If we got the chimney cleaned, we could light a fire downstairs, and put a kettle on the hook, and then we could have tea any time we wanted it," said Ellen. "And we could paint the walls and make it warm and cosy."

"I don't know," said Mrs Bailey doubtfully.

"We'll see to it, Mother," said Bella. "We'll put one of the beds in the downstairs room for you, and we'll have a little room each up here."

"It doesn't seem fair to you children to turf you out of your rooms," said Mrs Bailey. "If only we didn't have to do these things. Ever since your father died..."

"Don't start about Daddy again," said Ellen.

Mrs Bailey looked hurt. She had had a hard struggle since her husband died, trying to make ends meet. At first taking the big house by the seaside and letting rooms had seemed to answer all their problems, but now...

"Oh dear," she said.

"I'm sorry," said Ellen, who in her own way missed her father very much. "I didn't mean it like that."

There was an uncomfortable silence, which Bella broke. "That's all settled then," she said, in a determined voice. "If you two go inside and arrange the rooms for the Mooneys, I'll put this place to rights."

And so it was decided, or rather Bella decided it. With three extra rooms there was space to fit in the Mooneys, though the pair who wore pyjamas kept insisting that they would have been better off in their tent. They had been sleeping in the tent when the minibus was stolen, and with it went their clothes. All the others had risen early, because the bus was cold. They went for a walk on the sandhills, and when they got back there were Douglas and Thomas in their

15

pyjamas, convinced that the family had gone off without them. Douglas and Thomas were indignant, but not so indignant as the others were, when they realized what had happened.

"But we were parked beside your tent!" said Mary Mooney, the oldest girl. "Didn't you hear anything?"

Douglas and Thomas had heard nothing.

"Hopeless!" said Violet.

"Kids!" said Paul.

"I would have leapt on the thieves and overpowered them!" said Terence.

"Shut up, Terence!" said everyone.

And so they came to Bon Vista.

In Bon Vista, Ellen had gone to the loft to fetch the iron bedsteads. It proved easy enough to get the bed-ends and irons down the stairs, but the springs and mattresses were another matter. Every time she tried to move a mattress, it would swing back at her, and tangle her up. She was in the middle of telling one of the mattresses what she thought of it when a tall pale Mooney appeared on the stairs. "Can I help?" he said. "I heard you cursing."

"I wasn't," said Ellen.

"Perhaps it only sounded like it. I'm Paul Mooney. You are one of the landlady's lot, aren't you?"

Ellen didn't like being called "one of the

landlady's lot" but she did want the mattress moved.

"Yes," she said. "Could you take that end, please, I'm kind of tangled up in it at the moment!"

They made it down the stairs without breaking anything and out into the yard.

"Were you going to burn it, or shall I leave it beside the bins?" said Paul.

Ellen took this in. The mattress did look the worse for wear.

"Just leave it here," she said.

Four more trips up the stairs brought down the remaining odds and ends of the three beds.

"Thank you very much," said Ellen.

"Not at all," said Paul.

There was a lengthy pause. Ellen was anxious to get him out of the back yard, so that she could move the mattresses across to the back house without his seeing. Paul was quite prepared to be sociable.

"Do you like living here?" he said.

"It's all right," said Ellen.

"Is there much to do?"

"Enough," said Ellen, who never had any spare time to do things, and felt bitter about it.

"Where should I go, then?" asked Paul.

Anywhere out of my way, thought Ellen, but she said: "You could go and putt."

"What?" said Paul.

"*Putt*," said Ellen, witheringly. "With a stick, and a ball."

"At the Golf Course?" said Paul.

"The Golf Course is Members only," Ellen said. "Anyone knows that."

"Anyone who lives here does," Paul said, pushing the hair out of his eyes. It was a cabbage crop, and seemed to have been cut by someone using a pie dish, and shears ... if it ever has been cut, she thought.

"You might be better off at the Crazy Golf," she said, unkindly. She was losing patience with Paul wondering what to do, when she had to start the washing up and Bella was waiting for the beds.

"I can take a hint," said Paul, suddenly turning on his heel and going back into the house. Ellen was left feeling nasty.

"Silly ass!" she grumbled.

She hurried out to the back house.

"If you've come to help, help," said Bella. "If you've come to talk, go away!"

Ellen stayed and helped after a fashion.

"I wonder what it's like to be one of eleven children?" she said. "I'd love to…"

"Curiosity," said Bella.

"Why not? Why shouldn't I wonder?"

"Because you always want to know about

everything, Ellen," Bella said. "Why can't you just let well alone?"

"I was only *wondering*," said Ellen, in an aggrieved voice.

"I've had enough of your wondering," said Bella. "Do you remember the time you only *wondered* what it would be like to watch tadpoles turning into frogs?"

"I forgot about them," Ellen said.

"And we had frogs all over the house for weeks!" said Bella. "Then there was the time you wanted to know how the piano worked…"

"That was when I was small," said Ellen. "I wouldn't take a piano to pieces now … and if I did, I bet I'd be able to fix it anyway. I bet I could. I wonder if I could find out how a real piano tuner…"

"No," said Bella. "You couldn't. You're too curious by half. Curiosity killed the cat."

"It hasn't killed me yet," said Ellen.

Bella returned to her labours. Cleaning up the back house was one of the things they had planned to do when they first came to Bon Vista, but the boarding-house kept them so busy that the plans they had made for the back house were just plans, and the back house remained somewhere where they put their bicycles, or occasionally took refuge when people got on their nerves.

"There!" said Bella, looking proudly at the iron bedstead which she had chosen for herself. "That looks splendid!"

Ellen poked her head around the door. "I've got mine up, too, and I've put the mattress on."

"Give me a hand with mine," said Bella. Together they heaved the mattress on to the bed. It spread over the edges a bit, and there were several lumps, but it was a mattress. Ellen flopped down upon it and lay looking at the ceiling.

"'Up!" said Bella. "We're not finished yet."

"I know," said Ellen, resting on her elbow, and picking at the mattress, from which red fibres poked. "I was just thinking…"

"What about?"

"About Daddy," she said.

"Oh," said Bella.

"I don't really remember him," said Ellen. "I sort of do, and I sort of don't."

"He was nice," said Bella. "And you were very small when he died, Ellen."

"I wish I had known him properly," said Ellen. "I'd like to talk about him sometimes, with Mother, but somehow I can't seem to."

"I know," said Bella, sadly.

Ellen sat up on the bed and made herself smile. "I think he would have liked this house. It has a family feel about it. I bet there was a proper family here, with lots of children. I bet they played in the Demesne like we do, and up around the Lodge…"

"I don't think they'd have done that," said Bella. "After all, the Duvaliers would still have been living at the Lodge. It's just a ruin now, but I bet they didn't let the people from the cottages play around their front door."

"It must have been lovely," said Ellen. "Imagine living in a big white house amongst the trees like that, with the mountains behind you and the Lawn Field in front, running down to the sea. I wish I'd been a Duvalier."

"I'd rather be a Bailey," said Bella.

"I'd like to be rich," said Ellen. "I wonder what it is like, being rich?"

"I'd rather be a Bailey than a Mooney, anyway," said Bella.

"So would I," said Ellen. "I couldn't stand being a Mooney, there are so many of them."

"Eleven is too many," said Bella.

"One of them helped with the beds," said Ellen. "Oh … and the one called Terence put shrimps down the lavatory."

"He sounds a charmer!" said Bella.

"If the rest are like that…" said Ellen.

"I bet they are," said Bella. "They look it."

"I vote we have nothing to do with them," said Ellen. "We'll have our own house out here, and just visit Bon Vista. They can amuse themselves."

A shriek of laughter echoed from the yard. The Mooneys seemed to be good at amusing themselves.

"This is a better house, anyway," said Bella. "It may be smaller, but it's been here longer."

"I wonder who used to live here?" Ellen said, lying back on the bed and gazing up at the rafters.

The candle flickered by the bedside, throwing the shadow of Ellen's book against the underside of the slates.

It was past midnight.

The back house was noisy. Every time Bella moved in the room across the landing, the beams creaked.

Maybe I'll come through the ceiling on top of Mother, Ellen thought.

She had fixed a candle in a milk-bottle, which she'd placed on top of an orange-box beside the bed.

The wind rattled the window.

It was such a small house that it was difficult to believe that people had lived there, drinking, eating and sleeping. She lay in the upstairs room and thought about it. Her bed was set against the wall by the door, so that she could sit up without banging her head, for the rafters sloped down to about a foot above the floor. If she looked sideways she could see through the window. She had left her toilet things on the window-sill, with a water-jug and a bowl rescued from the loft in Bon Vista. She could be completely independent of Bon Vista, if she wanted to be.

She liked the back house better than Bon Vista.

Bon Vista was ... too big! It was full of stairs and landings and corridors and rooms, all needing constant attention. All the ceilings were high, with plaster mouldings of angels with harps, and brown and yellow flowery wallpaper which they couldn't afford to replace.

We could paint this house, she thought.

She sat up.

"Bella?" she called softly. "Are you awake?"

"Yes. What do you want?"

"We could paint these rooms, couldn't we?"

"Oh, go to sleep," said Bella.

Ellen lay back on her lumpy bed.

She lay still with her head cushioned on the pillow.

She liked the back house. She would make it live again.

She went to sleep watching the sky through the window. The stars were stabs of light against a dark blue cloth, and the moon was yellow and round.

In the still of the night, the only sound was a gentle ticking.

CHAPTER 2

When Ellen woke up in the morning, the first thing she saw was the window.

Through it she could see the back wall of Bon Vista, and the window of the back bedroom ... and *nothing else*.

No sky.

Just the grey wall and the rose which grew across the window.

CHAPTER 3

The morning began with a bang, which was the front door of Bon Vista closing, and a crash as the person who had closed it tripped over the milk-bottles in the porch.

Ellen, who was in the kitchen, was first into the hall and out to the front, closely followed by Bella and Mrs Bailey, but they were only just in time to see three hundred pounds worth of unpaid bill disappearing up the road, in the shape of the Smyths, who had complained about soft eggs and hard beds all week. They had made an early start to avoid paying their bill.

"It's such a mean thing to do," said Bella. "It isn't as if we had a lot of money to spare."

"We should tell the police," said Ellen, but she knew that that would be no use. If the Smyths were going to leave without paying their bill they probably weren't called Smyth at all, and they certainly wouldn't live at the posh address they had written in the guest-book.

"Regard me as screaming and cursing," said Bella glumly. Mrs Smyth owed her fifty pence, borrowed from the telephone box the night before when she "Just ran a bit short of change, dear." The fifty pence would have to be replaced, and Bella knew whose pocket-money it would come from.

"I'll make a cup of tea," said Mrs Bailey, turning from the door. She wore large red carpet slippers constructed on the scale of the *Titanic* but less sinkable, for they had carried her through pools and puddles and even, on this occasion, spilt milk.

There was a lot of spilt milk.

"I'll bet Spitting Hector did it deliberately," said Bella, with feeling. Spitting Hector had been the smallest Smyth. All he ever did was spit. He was a World Champion spitter, or he would have been if there had been a World Championship.

They turned to go into the kitchen and, as the door opened, a small cat slipped out, with a silly grin on its face.

"Oh, my goodness!" cried Mrs Bailey, and she disappeared to the back quarters to see what had happened to the sardines.

"Who owns that?" asked Ellen, pointing at the cat.

"I don't know," said Bella. "How about the Belshaws in number thirteen?"

There was a howl from the kitchen and the cat dived for the stairs.

The working staff of Bon Vista retreated to join the proprietor in a mourn-the-sardines cup of tea, and told themselves the unending saga of Guests We Have Known And Their Awful Ways. There had been many of them, from The Man Who Kept His Sausages For God to The Woman Who Slept Under The Bed, also starring, last but by no means least, The Man Who Put His Hair On The Bedpost. It was a wig, but it gave Mrs Bailey a nasty turn.

"Talking about nasty turns," said Ellen, "a funny thing happened to me last night," and she told them the story of the moon at the window.

"So what?" said Bella.

"So you can't see the sky from my window, let alone the moon! You can only see the back of Bon Vista," said Ellen.

There was a pause.

"If it was anybody else, I'd want to know what they'd been drinking," said Bella. "But as it's you, Ellen, I suppose it's about par for the course!"

"Oh, it wasn't just me! It really happened!"

Bella looked down her nose at her sister.

Mrs Bailey munched her toast and thought about her blue rinse. To be or not to be? She couldn't make up her mind, so she started to think about her daughters. Bella was too fat.

Ellen had too many notions, distinctly too many notions.

She never knew what Ellen would think of next.

Ellen had ambitions. She was going to keep more pigs than Billy Catchpole, be a world-famous actress, nurse the very handsome rich wounded, be a ballet dancer ... and not just a ballet dancer, *the* ballet dancer, Eleonora Von Baileyovska of the Garden. Eleonora Von Baileyovska was nothing if she was not light-footed, but her twinkling feet were in danger of being worn down to the knee-caps running up and down the stairs at Bon Vista.

"Don't make faces," said Ellen. "If I say I saw the moon, I saw the moon."

"With a cow jumping over it?" sighed Bella.

"That isn't funny, Bella," said Mrs Bailey.

"I thought it was," said Bella.

"Well, it wasn't," said Mrs Bailey, who was in no mood to see jokes. Bella and Ellen were enjoying the novelty of the back house, but from her point of view it was draughty, and she didn't mean to spend another night wondering if the roof was going to fall in on top of her. The disappearance of the Smyths left number seven vacant, and Mrs Bailey had not replaced the Vacancies card in the window. One night in the back house was more than enough.

Twenty breakfasts later, when the last Mooney had munched the last piece of marmalade on toast and Harold had spilled his cup of milk over Terence, Bella and Ellen retired to the back house.

"Now we'll have it all to ourselves," said Bella, as they took down their mother's bed. "We can put some chairs in here, and I'll bring out my radio."

Then they talked about paint.

White for the downstairs room.

Red and white for the stairs, red for the walls, white for the banisters.

"Blue in my room," said Ellen.

"Red in mine," said Bella.

"To match your fat cheeks," said Ellen, getting her own back for the cow.

Bella was *plump*, not *fat*, at least that was the way that Mrs Bailey put it, but either way didn't please Bella. The trouble had begun with toffee-apples. A very tiny Bella had found them irresistible, and the sweet tooth she acquired eating them had lasted her down the years. Now Bella could hardly look a toffee-apple in the face without thinking dark thoughts, but she still ate them.

"I'm off to buy paint," Bella said, and flounced out of the back house.

Ellen didn't mind.

She climbed the staircase slowly, seeing it

white, and the wall red. If they could get the chimney cleaned and light a fire in the hearth, there would be red flickers of flame dancing around the room at night. They could sit down there and toast soda bread at the fire, and have a kettle boiling on the hob ... and lots of hot butter ... except that it would have to be margarine, used sparingly. Butter was only for the paying guests.

She went into her own room.

With blue walls, and the window-frame painted white, and the bed the same, and a chair, and a table, and ... but there she stopped. They had already worked out the cost of the paint, and it was going to take care of nearly all their savings.

She sat on the bed and looked out of the window.

The business about seeing the moon and the sky annoyed her. She must, she supposed, have been asleep ... and yet she was almost certain that she hadn't been.

She lay down on the bed, to check if it was possible to see the sky from any other angle, but it wasn't. Could the sky have been reflected in the window of the back bedroom?

But she knew that that wasn't the answer. She had seen the dark blue sky, like a velvet cloth. She had seen the moon, and the stars.

She lay back on the pillow.

"I don't know," she said. "I don't understand."

Soon she fell asleep.

To cope with twenty-odd breakfasts Bella and Ellen had to get up at five o'clock in the morning. It was small wonder that she was tired.

She dreamed of the room downstairs, with a fire in the hearth, and an empty chair pulled up beside it.

It was a strange, sad dream. She was coming down the stairs into the room, and there was something that she wanted to do, but could not. It was to do with the room, and the chair ... especially the empty chair. She came down into the room and stood by the chair. There was a short-bladed knife by the fireside, and she bent and touched it ... and she knew *that it was time to go...*

"Spuds to peel, lazybones!" said Bella, shaking her by the shoulder.

Ellen did not know how long the dream had lasted. She followed Bella downstairs, blinking in the sunlight that poured into the room.

"What is the matter?" said Bella. "You've gone pale."

"I don't know," said Ellen, standing on the stair, where she had stood in the dream. "I don't know what's come over me."

"You must know!"

"I don't, I … well, for a moment there I felt … I felt as if I was someone else. I had a dream … you wakened me out of it. I was coming down the stairs … and for a moment I felt the dream had been true … only it wasn't. I was me … awake."

"What were you doing in the dream?" asked Bella.

"I had to go somewhere. I had to leave here."

"Go *where*?"

But Ellen didn't know.

There was no time for talk after that, for the hour had come for Eleonora Van Der Bailey, Cordon Bleu chef of Ireland's Premier Boarding-House, to busy herself in the kitchen at Bon Vista doling out cabbage, bacon and potatoes à la Ballaghbeg on umpteen dishes, followed by umpteen plates of stewed prunes, umpteen pots of tea, and umpteen biscuits. As the food went out of the kitchen, the dishes came back in, plates, spoons, cups, jugs, mugs and crumpled serviettes, not to mention a cat's dish which had somehow appeared on the list after the sardine breakfast. Every single thing had to be washed down to the last Apostle spoon, counted, and replaced in the appropriate tray.

"I'm killed dead!" said Bella, taking off her shoes, and wiggling her toes as she stretched back.

The bell rang.

Bella put on her shoes and disappeared into the dining-room, where Terence Mooney made *the* joke about her name. Bella marked him down for punishment. He was the medium Mooney with the red hair. A blood-feud was declared.

She put five extra teaspoons full of sugar in his cup.

She removed the biscuits from his side of the table to a place beside his sister Mary, who ran a sort of police force for the persecution of Terence.

He raised his cup. He took a sip.

Bella watched him, gloating.

"Could I have some more sugar, please?" he said, grinning at her.

Bella didn't grin back!

It was half-past three before the painting of the back house could begin, and at half-past four they had to stop to have their own tea, and prepare High Tea for the guests.

It was eight o'clock before they managed to escape from Bon Vista and find their way through the knee-high grass to the back house.

"I was talking to Billy Catchpole at the butcher's," said Bella. "He says that the road used to run through here, before our houses were built. He says if we dug down here we'd find cobbles. He says he had to give up trying to plant things in part of his garden because of them. He ended up building a pigsty instead."

"I've never heard of people having back houses before," Ellen said. "It seems a funny idea."

Bella shrugged. "I suppose that, instead of pulling the old houses down when they changed the line of the road, they built the new ones in front of the old, like Bon Vista. Some of the old houses were pulled down later, and some of them were used for hens, or garden sheds … or just left empty, like ours."

They both liked painting. It was interesting to see the paint go on, and watch the change in colour. Some bits were difficult, where the plaster had broken away, or on the stone mantle, where someone had carved a bird. But the wood on the stairs and the window-frames was easy, and they had done a lot of work before the light went.

"Tea," said Bella.

"If we had the chimney cleaned, we could boil our water on the fire," said Ellen. "I wonder if I had a brush…"

"No," said Bella.

"I'm going to try," said Ellen defiantly.

"On your own head be it," said Bella.

Ellen got out the yard brush and stuck it up the chimney.

A lot of dirt came down and, as Ellen was

holding the yard brush, most of it fell on top of her.

"Told you so," said Bella, as Ellen spluttered round the room. "Here, keep away from my clean paint! You and your 'I wonders'."

"It's in my eyes. I can't see."

"I'll get my hanky," said Bella. Carefully, she wiped the soot and grime from her sister's face.

"You look like a zebra," she said.

Ellen was not amused.

Her clothes were covered in soot and dirt, and her hair was full of it.

"I'll bring you out some water in a jug," said Bella. "I don't think you should go into the house looking like that ... Mother mightn't be pleased."

She disappeared into the garden and Ellen sat down to wait for her.

She opened the door.

It was a warm evening, and she felt sleepy.

Half-doors are nice, she thought, leaning on it and swinging gently. Down the centre panel of the door someone had carved four flowers. They were delicately worked and very real looking.

She stepped outside.

In the Demesne behind her a bird was calling.

She sat down on the grass. The painting had taken more out of her than she had expected. Every muscle in her body seemed to be sore.

Where was Bella?

What was keeping her?

Oh, hurry up, Ellen thought, picking at a daisy.

The bird stopped singing.

Ellen looked round.

There was a man standing at the half-door of the back house. He was white-haired, his shoulders drooping.

He wore a leather jerkin.

He was looking at her. He looked as if he was going to speak. He put out his hand...

Then her head seemed to spin ... she heard the bird sing ... the scene before her grew hazy ... she closed her eyes involuntarily ... opened them again...

He was gone. She was sitting on the grass, gazing at the open door of the back house, which was just as she had left it.

There was no one there.

She closed her eyes again.

It had been an odd feeling, lying there looking at him and feeling ... feeling *as though she was someone else.*

"I must have imagined it ... but I did see..."

But.

CHAPTER 4

The queer feeling stayed with her, but she didn't tell Bella about it. She couldn't be quite certain why she didn't tell Bella ... it seemed a very personal thing, something that was meant for her, and her alone.

When she had scrubbed the soot and dirt off her head and shoulders and completed the few remaining jobs that had to be done in Bon Vista, she was ready to go back to the house again to see if ... well, not to see if anything in particular ... but to see what would happen next.

"Curiosity!" she murmured to herself, reprovingly. She half didn't believe what had happened to her, but only half didn't believe ... the other half, the believing half, wanted to know more. She was afraid, but not only afraid. "Curiosity!" she muttered again, and that about summed it up.

But she had to bottle up her curiosity, for Mr and Mrs Mooney had gone out, and Ellen was despatched to tell Sally and Anna, the two youngest Mooneys, a bedtime story.

"What sort of story do you like?" she asked Anna, who was curled up beside her sister in the big double bed which normally belonged to Mrs Bailey.

"Bloody and gooey," said Anna, but Sally shook her head. "A nice story," she insisted.

"A nice bloody, gooey story," said Anna firmly.

"I'll tell you a story about here, shall I?" said Ellen.

"Is it bloody and gooey?" said Anna.

"Little girls aren't supposed to like bloody and gooey stories," objected Sally.

"I do," said Anna.

"It's a bloody story, but not very gooey," said Ellen. "You get right down beneath the blankets and I'll tell it."

"Good," said Anna, wriggling down beneath the sheets, and popping her thumb into her mouth.

"She's not supposed to suck her thumb!" Sally objected, as Ellen pulled the coverlet firmly up to the two small brown faces.

"Never mind," said Ellen. "This is the story of Peadar McShane."

"Who was he?" said Anna, sitting up. "Who..."

"Down," said Ellen firmly.

The two Mooneys were very good, once the story had got going. It was a story Ellen knew off by heart, because Bella had told it to her often. They liked the bit about McShane's ride along the coast road and how the soldiers waited for him in the darkness.

"How could they see him?" said Anna. "Did they have torches?"

"There was a lovely full moon," said Ellen.

It was a nice story to tell, because she could add all sorts of bits to it about the chase along the cliffs, and McShane's horse rearing in the moonlight, as he faced the storming sea.

"He stood on the cliff, at bay, beside his horse, with the relentless pursuers galloping toward him. He drew his sword," said Ellen. "The moonlight flashed on the blade, then … what do you think happened then?"

"He cut them all to pieces with his sword," said Anna.

"I bet he didn't," said Sally. "I bet they cut him to pieces."

"You're both wrong," said Ellen. "He thrust his sword into the ground, said a prayer, and jumped off the cliff, right down into the pounding waves below, and he was drowned."

"Is that all?" said Anna, sounding disappointed.

"Not quite," said Ellen, and the two little girls

settled down beneath the coverlet again. She spun out the story of Peadar McShane's sweetheart as far as it would go. "Each evening she walked by the cliffs, to the place where her lover had died."

"What's a lover?"

"The man she was going to marry," said Ellen. "She was heartbroken because she had lost her true love. And then one day, as she stood looking down at the sea, she heard a strange voice whisper to her. It said:

> O come to me, beloved,
> And stay here, by my side.
> O come to me, beloved,
> At the turning of the tide."

"Ghosts!" said Anna, with a shiver. "Is it ghosts?"

"It was a ghost," said Ellen. "The ghost of her true love, calling to her from the waves."

"Oh," said Anna.

"And she cast off her cloak and walked to the edge of the cliffs, and she said:

> I'll come to you, beloved,
> I'll stay by your side.
> I'll come to you, beloved,
> At the turning of the tide.

"And then she undid her hair, so that it flowed out in the wind behind, and she jumped off the cliffs into the storming water below, and she was never seen again."

Sally had gone to sleep.

"Is that all?" said Anna, with a yawn.

"Not absolutely all," said Ellen, "because someone cut the words the lovers had spoken on a rock, and they put it beside the place where they drowned, and it's there to this very day. There is a great slit in the side of the cliff with a bridge over it, and they call it Peadar's Leap, after Peadar McShane, and people go there to troth their love."

"What's troth?" said Anna.

"Pledge," said Ellen.

"The fish would eat them, wouldn't they?" said Anna.

"I expect they went to heaven," said Ellen.

"Their souls would," said Anna, in a very serious voice. "But I expect the fish would chew their bodies up into little pieces."

"Well, maybe," said Ellen reluctantly.

"So it *is* a bloody, gooey story," said Anna, with satisfaction.

"If you like," said Ellen.

When she finally managed to escape from the bedroom, she told her mother about the demand for bloody, gooey stories. "I had to agree that they got eaten by fish!" she said. "I think that's horrid, don't you?"

"It's a peculiar story to tell children, anyway," said Mrs Bailey reprovingly. "Whatever put it in your head?"

41

"I don't know," said Ellen. "It came to me ... I'd no real reason. I suppose I remembered it because of the verse in the rock, you know the one ... 'the turning of the tide'."

"I see," said Mrs Bailey.

"I wonder who heard it?" said Ellen. "I mean someone must have because they were both dead, weren't they? I wonder..."

"Stop wondering," said Mrs Bailey. "You'll wonder your head off, one day."

"Maybe I will," said Ellen.

The verse stayed in her mind for the rest of the evening, rhyming away at the back of everything she did.

"I can't get the old thing out of me!" she grumbled to Bella, as they crossed to the back house.

Bella went up the stairs to her own room, but Ellen stayed below, drawing the curtains.

As she turned from the window, the light of the candle glistened on something in the hearth, amid the pile of rubbish and soot which had come down on her head. She crossed the room and knelt beneath the carved bird.

She poked the something. Metal ... and wood.

Then she picked it up, getting her hand soot-blackened in the process.

It was a flintlock pistol.

"Where did you get that?" said Bella, standing

by the foot of the stairs.

"It must have fallen down the chimney, when I stuck the brush up," Ellen said.

"You're lucky it didn't brain you! What is it?"

"It's a pistol, I think, an old one. Or what's left of one."

Bella took it from her.

"That bit looks like silver," she said. "But the barrel's rotted through. It must be very old."

"Funny place to keep a pistol," said Ellen. "I bet it's worth a lot of money."

Bella shook her head. "I don't think so," she said.

"There are lots of these about, and this one is in a terrible state. Most of it has rotted away."

"Well, it's very interesting anyway," said Ellen, protecting her discovery from criticism. She took it back, and held the candle close to it, to inspect it.

"I *expect* it is very *very* old," she said.

Bella smiled. "We'll ask Mr Carncross at the station. He knows about that sort of thing."

"Y ... e ... s," said Ellen warily. She knew Mr Carncross. So few people came to talk to him that he made every conversation an event.

"You can take it to him tomorrow morning, after we've done breakfast," said Bella.

"I suppose so," said Ellen. "I wonder why it was hidden up the chimney in the first place?"

"Someone didn't want it found."

It was a practical answer, but not the answer Ellen was looking for, which had to do with duels on the sand, or midnight rides to stop beautiful duchesses being carried off by highwaymen.

"I know *that*," Ellen said impatiently.

"Well then," said Bella.

Ellen looked at the hearth and looked at the chimney. She ducked down and put her head inside. "I wonder…"

"Ellen!" Bella said.

"I bet I could get up the chimney," said Ellen eagerly. "I might find all sorts of things up there."

"And you might not," said Bella.

Ellen looked at Bella, and looked at the chimney. She was itching with curiosity. It was all very well saying she shouldn't be curious and that curiosity killed the cat … it didn't make her *feel* she shouldn't be curious.

"I'll just go up a *little* bit," she said.

"Not in those clothes," said Bella, who had seen the effects of soot on one set of Ellen's clothing.

"I'll put on my painting things," said Ellen.

When she was ready, she ducked under the mantel, and peered up into the darkness. "I bet I find treasure," she said. "Or something like that. I wonder whether…"

"I wonder whether you'll get stuck," said Bella.

"There are sort of footholes in the sides," said the muffled voice inside the mantelpiece. "I think I can … yes … I can. I wonder what they were for?"

"That's obvious, isn't it?" said Bella, who was both tired and at the same time alarmed that Ellen's curiosity was going to get her into another mess. It was always a short step from Ellen "wondering" about something to Ellen trying to find out. There was no stopping her. Once she wondered, *she had to know*.

A muffled shout came from the chimney, together with some soot, rubble and plaster and the dirt of ages.

Ellen's legs and feet disappeared.

"What's up there?" said Bella, keeping clear of the debris.

"A ledge," said Ellen. Then there was a pause. "It does get into your throat, this stuff." Another pause. "Nothing on it, though."

"Where's Ellen?" said Mrs Bailey, peering round the door. "She hasn't put the milk-crate out."

Bella could have said: "Up the chimney," but she thought her mother might not approve.

"I don't know," she said, thinking that she was being strictly honest. She knew Ellen was up the

45

chimney, but not precisely *where* up the chimney.

"Isn't she here?" said Mrs Bailey. "At this time of night she should be."

"She isn't exactly not here," said Bella.

"She isn't exactly here, either," said Mrs Bailey, in a withering voice. "Where…"

The question was answered from the fireplace.

"Hello, Mother," said the soot-ball.

"Ellen!"

"I just thought … I'd take a look up the chimney," said Ellen, finishing her sentence in the uncomfortable knowledge of the doom to come.

"Get out of there this minute!"

It was a chastened and well-washed Ellen who returned to the back house, flesh tingling, from a scrubbing which had not, perhaps, been as tender as it might have been.

Bella was asleep.

"Muggins is me," said Ellen, closing the door of her own room.

She was disappointed about the chimney. There had been nothing up there but an empty stone ledge. It was a curious place to keep a pistol.

She went to the window and looked out hopefully.

All she could see was the back of Bon Vista and the lighted window of the back bedroom.

No sky, no moon.

She didn't feel like going to sleep.

"Letters," she said to herself.

She got out her writing-case from the mound of belongings she had brought out from her room in Bon Vista, which was now occupied by three of the Mooneys. She pulled the chair she had kidnapped from the garden-shed up to the window, and used the sill to rest the paper on. Then she got out her pen and started to write.

But somehow she didn't get very far with the letter.

It was to be to her friend Lucie Catchpole, the pig-man's daughter, who was with the Guides in Scotland. It was a "Wish I was there" letter, and they are always difficult to write, not like the "Wish you were here" sort.

Eventually she gave up.

I ought to be sleepy, she thought. I've got to get up in the morning, and I'll be dead!

But she wasn't sleepy. I wonder if they'll get their minibus back?

I wonder if they've thought of calling it a "Mooney Bus".

I wonder if Mother would let me keep this room, after they've gone?

I wonder…

She was busy thinking of things to wonder about, when something peculiar happened.

One moment she was sitting with her pen poised between her fingers and the next...

...the pen twitched and then...

...started to write!

She could feel it move between her fingers, feel her hand moving with it ... but she was not directing it.

It wrote in a neat copperplate hand, slowly.

M..Y....N..A..M..E.....I..S

She gripped the pen, and the writing stopped.

My name is, she read.

Then she said it out loud: "My name is!"

"Your name is Ellen, and will you for goodness' sake get into your bed and go to sleep," said Mrs Bailey, poking her head round the door. "You've got to get up in the morning, and for once I'm doing the wondering ... wondering how you're going to do it, if you don't get some sleep!"

"Oh, but...!"

"Don't argue!" said Mrs Bailey. "Not if you value your life!"

Ellen got into bed.

When Mrs Bailey had gone back to her room in Bon Vista, Ellen got her writing-case out again. She sat up in bed and held the pen patiently for ages, but it would not write.

48

"I wonder what makes it work?" she said to herself. "I wonder ... I wonder what is happening to me?"

She went to sleep, lulled by a faint ticking sound which came, and went, and came again as she drifted further into sleep.

CHAPTER 5

Mr Carncross kept the newsagent's stall in the Railway Station.

When the trains came, he had to rush about a lot, selling papers to two or three or four people at once, and all with only one pair of hands, and a weak head for mathematics ... when the trains *came* ... but the trains didn't come any more.

The Railway Company had taken away the railway track and the silver-painted clock which, like a pocket-watch, dangled from an orna-mental support above the entrance to Platform One. They had taken the brass sign from the door of the Station Master's Office, and rolled up the coconut matting in the waiting-rooms. They knocked down the Railway Cottages, and sold the marshalling yard to a property developer. Now there were bungalows where the trains used to be, complete with central heating and fishponds.

The station was empty, even a little eerie. The

Bus Company had taken over the ticket office as a Parcel Centre; apart from that, the only activity was when Mr Carncross sold a paper, which didn't happen very often. He sat in a wooden stall which was painted a yellowy brown, with old cigarette advertisements covering the scuffed wood at the front, and yellow curtains pulled across the window at the back. He had a tall stool with a leather seat and he had taken to sitting on it with his right elbow on the thin display of month-old magazines on the counter and his left elbow on the window ledge at the back.

If he turned his head he could see, through the chink in the curtains, the back gardens of the bungalows where the "Up" line to Belfast had been. If he turned his head the other way he could see that no customers were coming. So he looked straight in front of him at the side wall of the stall, and saw it all the way it used to be.

"Mr Carncross," said Ellen.

No reply.

Was he dead?

"Hello, Mr Carncross!" said Bella, turning up the volume.

He wasn't dead.

He turned his head and smiled.

"The wee Baileys," he said.

At another time and with another person, Bella would have been huffed about being classed as a

51

"wee Bailey". She wasn't small, she was large, though not as large as she thought she was.

"Thought you were dead, Mr Carncross," said Ellen cheerfully. She had a habit of saying things that might annoy people, without thinking first. Bella took a quick look at Mr Carncross to see how he would take it.

"I'm not," he said.

He was happy in his stall. It was warm and quiet and he was hardly ever disturbed by customers with their bothersome change. He had plenty of time to enjoy remembering things.

"I'm just waiting for the trains," he said, with a smile, tapping his finger on a day-old newspaper.

Bella looked at Ellen.

Ellen looked at Bella.

Bella shrugged. If they didn't do something quickly they might well be in for a dose of his reminiscences.

Bella was about to put the package containing what was left of the flintlock pistol on his *Woman's Realm* when Ellen said: "There aren't any trains, are there?" in a matter-of-fact way.

"I suppose you can't see them," he said. "But I can, if I let myself."

"You mean you can *actually* see things that used to be, and aren't here any more?" asked Ellen cautiously.

He smiled but said nothing.

"Send for the man with the big white van!" muttered Bella under her breath.

Ellen persisted. "I'm interested, but I don't know what you mean."

"If you don't know what I'm talking about, I can't tell you!" he said.

"Screw loose!" muttered Bella.

He looked at her sharply.

Maybe he wasn't as deaf as he was supposed to be, she thought, and she felt herself blush. Deaf people always heard the things they weren't meant to.

The silence became uncomfortable. Bella took the package from Ellen and put it on the counter.

"We wanted you to take a look at that for us, please, Mr Carncross," she said.

"What's all this?" he said, untying the paper.

"A very *very* old pistol," said Ellen proudly, but he didn't seem to hear her.

"Well, I never," he said. "You have to have a fire-arms licence for this, you know."

"Oh dear," said Ellen, taken aback. "Do we really?"

"Not unless you're going to fire it off, and I don't think we could fire *that* off," said Bella, disdainfully.

"You're part right and part wrong," said Mr Carncross. "A pistol is a pistol, whether or not you mean to fire it. Even antique guns have to be licensed, because some of them could be used. But this one ... I don't know that one could really call it a pistol any more, do you?"

"I could," said Ellen.

They all looked at the pistol as it lay half on *Weekend* and half on a pile of *Ballaghbeg Observer*.

The silver mounting on the butt was green. The trigger and lock were badly corroded. The end of the barrel had broken off.

"I *suppose* I could, anyway," said Ellen, her confidence waning.

"Let me see now," said Mr Carncross, getting down from his stool. He bent beneath the counter and rummaged around, producing a spanner and a bicycle pump and four chessmen before he finally brought out a small yellow tin and extracted a lump of wadding, which he rubbed vigorously on the butt of the old pistol.

"There!" he said, putting it down.

Where he had rubbed, the silver gleamed like new.

"There's something on it!" exclaimed Ellen. "It's somebody's initials ... J.D."

"Who?" asked Bella.

"Duvalier," said Mr Carncross. "At least I expect so! It would make sense."

"Like the Lodge?" said Ellen.

"That's right," he said. "But there are no

54

Duvaliers there now, only Billy Catchpole's pigs." He turned the pistol over. "J.D. ... that would be John Duvalier. There were several Johns, the family seemed to like the name. How did you get this?"

Ellen explained about sticking the yard brush up the chimney, and the pistol falling down. "It must have just missed my head," she said.

"I must tell old John, if I see him," said Mr Carncross. "He doesn't get out and about much now, and he's poor as a church mouse."

"Does he live at the Lodge?" asked Ellen. "Imagine living up there, with no roof, and no glass in the windows and Billy's pigs sniffing round the door!"

"Not old John," said Mr Carncross. "Though come to think of it I don't know where he does live now. You want to be careful about him, he's not been treated very kindly by the world ... or at least he thinks so."

"What happened to him?" asked Ellen.

"Nosy!" said Bella.

"I like to know things," said Ellen. "What happened to him? Why is he poor as a church mouse? Why are church mice poor, anyway? I wonder..."

"You've wondered enough for one day," grumbled Bella, who began to feel that she was in for a long, long conversation.

"John lost a lot of money," said Mr Carncross. "I suppose you know what death duties are, do you? When rich people die, if they leave a lot of money, the government takes most of it."

"That doesn't seem fair," said Ellen. "It's their money."

"Oh, I think the idea is that the same families shouldn't remain rich for ever and ever, just because one of their ancestors did a lot of work. What happens usually is that rich people give their money away before they die, or tie it up in trusts and companies."

"I see," said Ellen.

"John Duvalier's father wasn't like that," said Mr Carncross. "He was *odd*, like John himself. He thought everyone was against him. So he held on to his money, and the result was that when he died the government took most of what he left. It's sad really, the family did a lot of good here at one time."

"What sort of thing did they do?" asked Ellen.

"Well, let me see ... the fishtraps, for one thing. They got them going. You know what I mean ... the big stone semi-circles of boulders on the beach? You can see them clearly at low tide."

"I don't believe anyone could trap fish in them," said Bella scornfully. "What a silly idea!"

"They didn't trap fish," said Mr Carncross. "No, the idea was that shellfish and sea creatures

56

would breed among the stones, and when the tide was in the fish would try to eat them. The fish traps were an enormous bait if you like, bringing the fish into the bay, where people could catch them."

"I wonder why they don't do it now?" said Ellen. "I wonder if I got a boat and went fishing there, would I catch anything now? I wonder…"

"What about our pistol?" said Bella, cutting her off in mid-sentence.

Ellen closed her mouth. Then opened it again. Then shut it. "Our pistol", indeed! Bella was always taking things over and running them.

"Is it worth any money?" Bella asked. "How much would I get for it?"

"We," said Ellen, under her breath.

He shook his head. "Not as it is," he said. "Oh, I suppose you could get something for the silver."

"*I*'d rather keep it, thank you," said Ellen firmly, just as Bella opened her mouth to speak.

Bella shut her mouth with a snap, like a fish catching a fly.

"You'll have to find the other one," said Mr Carncross.

"The other one?"

"This was a duelling pistol," he said. "They come in pairs."

They walked down the Main Street together.

"It might be *ours*," said Ellen, stretching a point. "But it certainly isn't *yours*. I found it. I don't mind sharing."

"You can keep the rotten old thing," said Bella.

"Fatty!" called Archie McCullough, as Bella and Ellen went past him.

Bella blushed to the roots of her hair, but she held her head high and said nothing.

"An *odd* thing happened to me last night," said Ellen, not quite knowing how to begin the story of the pen that wrote of its own accord.

"I can't help being fat, can I?" said Bella, with an outraged sniff.

Ellen concluded that this was not a question, and therefore did not require an answer.

"I was writing to Lucie Catchpole," she said. "I was in my own room, just sitting there, holding my pen and thinking when…"

"Am I *awfully* fat?"

"You aren't," said Ellen, not absolutely truthfully. "I was…"

"Yes, I am!"

"Not *very*," said Ellen.

"Very."

"Phyllis is fatter," Ellen pointed out, but this didn't cheer Bella up at all.

Phyllis was famous. She jumped off the high board in the swimming pool and there was such a big splash that someone called her "Atom Bomb" and the name had stuck, with several variations.

Bella looked at herself in the window of the greengrocer's shop which they were passing.

She saw an enormous Dumbo-like creature in a blue jersey with a blue-jeaned bottom that looked as if it might take off on its own.

That was what Bella saw, or what she made of what she saw.

Other people saw her differently. She looked what she was, a big girl with long wavy hair and red cheeks like apples and kind eyes ... very different from the Dumbo reflected in the shop window.

"I was telling you about last night..." Ellen began.

"I'm going to have an ice-cream to cheer myself up," Bella announced. "Coming?"

Ellen didn't think much of people who got upset because they were fat, and had to take ice-cream to comfort themselves.

She said so.

"So you *do* think I'm fat!" exclaimed Bella. "Well, in that case I'm not even going to talk to you!" And she tossed her head and walked away, into the ice-cream shop.

Ellen was left alone.

Not *very* alone.

There were lots of people on the Main Street

of Ballaghbeg, and lots more idling on Drumna Bridge, or walking about on the promenade.

Lots of people, but not her friends. Lucie and Belinda were with the Guides in Scotland, and Philomena had measles, and wasn't allowed out of bed.

Lots of people she could have talked to, if she'd wanted to, but she didn't.

She was sick of being bossed about by Bella, and at last she was doing something about it! Bella will just have to get used to me answering back when she tries something on! she thought.

She slouched along the promenade. Funny, how she'd imagined that old man at the door of the back house … there was something odd about the back house, something … just something. She could feel it in her bones.

Ellen turned across the grass. It was firm beneath her feet, for the summer had been a dry one. She could see Bon Vista over the bridge. A tall Victorian house, with lots of windows and a red pom-pom on top of the roof above the bay window, where sea-gulls sometimes sat.

"I like it here," she said to herself. "It's much better than Belfast…"

"Hello!" said the girl on the wall. "You're Ellen, aren't you? I'm Violet Mooney." She was short, brown, and smiling. She wore a frilly blue frock that looked two sizes too big for her.

60

Ellen was about to toss her head and walk by, and then she remembered that she was fighting with Bella, and the rest of her friends were in Scotland, or bed.

"Hello," she said.

"I'm waiting for Mary," Violet explained. "She's gone across to the shops."

Ellen got up on the wall. "Are you enjoying yourselves?" she said.

"Not much to do," said Violet.

"I could take you to some nice places," Ellen heard herself saying.

"Could you?"

"Yes."

They talked about possible places, and Ellen doodled in the dry sand on the promenade walk with the toe of her shoe. "At the turning of..."

She scrubbed it out! Not that old verse again!

"Peadar's Leap," she said. "That's the place. We'll bathe!"

At the same moment, Paul Mooney was buying a coffee for Bella. "Your sister has a sharp tongue, hasn't she?" he said, remembering the conversation about the putting.

"Very," said Bella with emphasis, but then she remembered that her sister was her sister. "She's not too bad, when you get used to her. She'd be all right, if she wasn't so nosy."

"Nosy?"

"Well, not *really* nosy, I suppose. But she always wants to know everything about everybody, and how things work and... Oh, I don't know. She's always *wondering* about this, that and the other ... she was wondering what it was like to be a Mooney, did you know that?"

"What did you decide?"

Bella grinned. "That it couldn't be very nice," she said, and then thought, helplessly, that that was the one thing she shouldn't have said.

"Oh?"

"Well, there are so many of you, aren't there?"

"I don't mind that," said Paul.

"I would. And I couldn't put up with that little brother of yours either."

When they had finished their coffee, they walked on down the street towards the funfair.

"Coming in?" said Paul. Bella nodded. She liked him. She hoped he liked her. If he didn't like her, he wouldn't be talking to her, would he? But then he didn't know anyone else. Still...

I bet he thinks I'm fat, she thought as she went through the archway and down the alley to the funfair. They passed between the roundabouts and the swing boats and he helped her up on to a broken part of the wall, where she sat with her back against a gnarled tree growing on the other side, with her hair blowing in the wind.

"You look pretty," he said, suddenly.

"Pretty fat," she said.

He shook his head. "Pretty."

Bella felt herself blushing and looked away. A dog was finding its way gingerly across the breakwater of the boating lake, stopping to sniff at piles of driftwood.

"What does your father do?" she asked, and then she grinned. "I sound like Ellen, don't I?"

"He's a draughtsman in the Aircraft Factory," said Paul. "Your father is dead, isn't he?"

"Yes," said Bella.

"Maybe I shouldn't have said that," he said.

"No ... I don't mind. I mean, well I do mind, but I don't, if you see what I mean."

"I know what you mean," he agreed, although he didn't really.

"Ellen is the one who misses him most," Bella said. "But then she doesn't remember him properly, she was too small when he died."

"Yes," said Paul.

"I'll have to go home now," she said, getting down from the wall. "Potatoes to peel."

"I'll come too," he said.

"To eat them," she grinned.

"Yes."

He helped her down from the wall. They walked towards the entrance of the funfair.

She was first through the entrance.

63

A horn blared, there was the sound of squealing brakes, and a blue minibus swerved across the road, narrowly missing the lamp-post on the other side, and pulled to a stop.

Bella was white in the face. The minibus had only missed her by inches.

"Are you all right?" Paul asked. "Here, that bus was going far too fast. I've a good mind to…"

The minibus engine started again, and the driver pulled swiftly back on to the road, and roared off.

"Without so much as stopping to see if you were all right!" said Paul, helping Bella on to the footpath.

"That was too close for comfort," Bella muttered, still feeling shaken. "He was going far too fast. He could have killed me. He … what's the matter?"

"That minibus…" said Paul. Then he shook his head. "It couldn't be … but just the same…?"

"Not yours? The one that was stolen?"

"They all look much the same. But the colour was right … and he wouldn't stop, would he? Not if it was stolen. He'd be too afraid of the police coming on the scene. I wish I'd got the number … then I would know."

"You should tell the police," said Bella.

"I've got nothing to tell them, have I?" said

Paul. "I wasn't really concerned about the minibus … I was worried about *you*. If I hadn't been, I would know…"

Worried about *me*, thought Bella.

I bet it *was* our bus, thought Paul.

CHAPTER 6

There had been a change in the atmosphere at Bon Vista.

Mrs Bailey noticed it, but didn't understand it. All of a sudden the Mooney clan were in favour.

First it was Ellen, who wanted to know if she could lend a pair of jeans to Violet Mooney. "Hers were stolen," Ellen explained. "Now she's wearing one of Mary's frocks, and it doesn't fit her."

"I see," said Mrs Bailey.

"She says they haven't got enough money for new ones," said Ellen. "Mary's clothes are frumpy, and Violet doesn't like them."

So Violet Mooney got the jeans.

"Do you like Paul?" asked Bella, who had carefully arranged events so that she was alone with her mother in the pantry.

"Paul?"

"Paul Mooney. The biggest boy, you *know*."

"I don't know if I do," said Mrs Bailey. "I can't tell one of them from another."

"He's the handsome-looking one," said Bella.

"I see," said Mrs Bailey gravely.

"And the thing is, he wants me to go to the fireworks display with him."

"I see," said Mrs Bailey.

"I wondered if you would mind?"

"Not a bit," said Mrs Bailey, only just managing to hide a grin.

So Bella had a boyfriend! When her daughter had gone out to the front, Mrs Bailey sat back in the kitchen, feeling nostalgic. I suppose I must be getting old! she thought, and it seemed a strange idea, for she felt young. "Bella, courting! How I wish … no." She got out of the kitchen chair, and went into the dining-room.

Four of the Mooneys were sitting on the sea wall. Paul, Violet, Mary and Anna. Ellen was with them, and Bella was beside the biggest boy. Bella was laughing, happy … but Ellen wasn't taking part in the group, she was gazing into the air in front of her, looking very serious indeed.

"I wonder what she's wondering about *this* time," Mrs Bailey said to herself.

Dinner came and went, and the two girls worked through it, without saying an unnecessary word to each other.

Ellen was tight-lipped and taking it out on the mashed potatoes.

Bella was cheerful, but kept looking as though butter wouldn't melt in her mouth.

"Everybody is behaving very oddly today," said Mrs Bailey, stroking the white cat which had turned up on her lap.

The cat had fallen on good times. It had been smuggled in in the first place by the young couple from Glasgow on the second floor, who couldn't bear to leave it at home. Following the sardine raid the cat had discovered where the food and warmth were and taken up residence forthwith, remaining there as long as the young couple were out of the house. When they came in, it disappeared. When they went out, it came trotting down the stairs again. Mrs Bailey, after her first feeble protests about the "no animals" rule, had decided that the rule *really* meant Alsatians and pet mice, and had insisted on feeding the cat on herring roes. As a result she was popular with both the cat and the young couple who, complete with a pair of two-year-old tartan twins, had been finding the smuggling of cat food up the stairs a trial.

"Sally Gilbert is getting married," said Bella.

"Who to?"

"A fishmonger from Ardglass with a big red mother," said Bella, grinning.

"A what?"

"She visited the Gilberts and she was all

dressed in red and Sally says she looked like a post-box with bows tied round it."

Mrs Bailey digested this.

Ellen tossed down the drying cloth. "Finished!" she exclaimed. "I must go and change."

"Change?" said Mrs Bailey. "But you look very nice!"

"Not for walking on the cliffs," said Ellen scornfully, and she waltzed out of the room.

Mrs Bailey looked after her in amazement. Ellen was not exactly well known for taking cliff walks.

"Along the cliffs?" said Mrs Bailey. "She's not going poetic this time, is she?"

"She's going out with Violet Mooney," said Bella. "Kids!"

"Aren't you going with them?"

Bella shook her head.

"Are you two having a quarrel?" said Mrs Bailey.

"Not what you'd call a quarrel exactly," said Bella. "Ellen gets on my nerves."

"What is it this time?"

"She says funny things keep happening in her room. First she saw the moon from her window when you can't … and now she says her pen writes on its own. I suppose she's having one of her notions, but I think it's about time she behaved normally like everyone else."

"Never mind," said Mrs Bailey. "She's just going through a stage, dear."

Ellen was in her room in the back house, changing into her bathing-costume. She put it on, then she slipped her jeans over the costume, and put a shirt on.

"I bet I look as fat as Bella!" she muttered, as she went into her sister's room to brush her hair. Picking up her sister's hairbrush, she turned toward the mirror...

Something odd was happening ... she felt as though suddenly, without any warning, everything had changed ... she put her hand to her face ... and the girl reflected in the mirror did the same ... of course she would ... she was only a reflection...

But the face in the mirror was not Ellen's.

Someone else looked back at her from the glass ... someone young, pale, crying...

And she, Ellen, was crying too ... and inside she was bewildered, lost, crowded ... as though someone else were crowding her out of her body, as though...

"*Ellen*?" Violet Mooney called from the foot of the stairs.

She was gazing at her own familiar face in the mirror. She was not crying, but on her cheek there glistened a single tear.

CHAPTER 7

Violet was waiting for Ellen, and so were three other Mooneys, and a tent.

"Oh!" said Ellen.

"We're coming too," said Terence.

"With our tent," said Thomas and Douglas.

"Hello," said Violet, ruefully. Then she blurted out: "I'm sorry about them, Mother said they had to come. At least she said I had to look after them, and that means they'll have to come."

"I can look after myself," said Terence, swinging a tent-pole carelessly around his head.

"Maybe we shouldn't go," Ellen said, but she saw Violet's face fall. "Oh, I suppose it will be all right, as long as they don't mind walking."

"We'll have to help them put their tent up," said Violet.

"You won't!" said Thomas firmly.

"This is Terence," said Violet, formally.

"I know about Terence," said Ellen. "Who are the other two?"

"Douglas," said Douglas.

"And Thomas," said Thomas. Then he added, very grandly, "I'm in charge of the tent."

The two tenters stood together, both of them clad in blue shorts which stopped just below the knee-cap.

Off the party went.

Ellen and Violet went in front. Douglas and Thomas came behind and Terence … well, one minute he was in front, being an ambush, and the next moment he was behind, throwing sea-weed at his brothers.

"If you don't stop it, I'll send you home," threatened Violet, removing a large piece of crab from her hair. It had been intended to hit Douglas on the ear, but Terence had missed.

"Sorry," he said, and promptly disappeared again, only to return with a dark and sticky mess on his hands.

"Tar!" he said triumphantly.

"You won't get that off easily," said Ellen.

But Terence didn't manage too badly. Part of it he rubbed off on the tent and then, when Douglas and Thomas turned to defend their property, he rubbed it off on them.

"That's nasty, Terence," Violet said. "You bully!"

Then Douglas poked Terence with the tent-pole.

"You'll all go home!" threatened Violet, desperately. "Mary can handle them, but I don't seem to have the knack," she confided to Ellen.

They went past the harbour and followed the road as it climbed along the cliffs. Looking back they could see the narrow ribbon of the town running around the bay, and then the distant sandhills, and beyond them again the lighthouse on Helier Point, jutting up from the dark rocks like a finger raised in warning.

"Ballaghbeg means the Narrow Pass in Irish," Ellen explained. "If you look at the way this road threads along the top of the cliff, with the sea on one side and the mountains rising steeply on the other, you'll see how the town got its name."

Violet wasn't sure that she liked the cliff road. The sea seemed to be very far below, and unfriendly.

"It's all right, we're going down now," said Ellen, opening the gate at the top of the Long Stair.

"No nonsense now," Violet warned the boys, as they started the lengthy descent. Douglas and Thomas were awed by the height, but Terence bounced about as if he wasn't three hundred steps up from the rocks below.

They came to the foot of the Long Stair and started along the narrow path cut out of the rock.

"Where do we bathe?" asked Terence.

"Not here anyway," said Violet with a shiver.

They came to a rope bridge, and Ellen got them to stand on it and look down at the water in the cut below... Thomas looked down, but shut his eyes firmly, on the theory that what he didn't see he wouldn't fall into.

"This is Peadar's Leap," Ellen explained, pointing down at the narrow channel in which the water frothed and churned. She turned round. "If you look there," she said, pointing at the cliff face, "you'll see that it becomes a cave, but only a foot or so wide."

"It's as if someone had cut a thin slice out of a cake," said Violet.

"At high tide there are all sorts of echoes," Ellen said.

"They say that the cave runs right inside the mountain. I think it's a creepy place. Lots and lots of people have drowned here."

"I wouldn't drown," said Terence. "I can swim like a fish."

"Shut up, Terence!" said Violet.

"I would swim and rescue myself," said Terence.

It was on the tip of Ellen's tongue to say that nobody else was likely to bother.

"It's more of a crack than a cave, really," said Violet, slowly.

"I bet there's treasure," said Terence. "I'm going down."

"Oh, no, you're not," said Ellen.

"Isn't there a way down?" said Violet. "It looks exciting."

"You can get across the rocks to the entrance, but there's no way in," said Ellen. "The waves would pluck you off the sides."

They followed the path from Peadar's Leap along to the point of the headland, and beyond it again to the bed of the Blue River.

"You bathe here," said Ellen, pointing to a pool by Slaughter Bridge. "Violet and I are going to the pool above."

"Can we put up our tent?" asked Thomas.

Violet agreed, and followed Ellen as she scrambled up the rocky bed of the river till they reached the Blue Pool.

"This is a good pool for bathing, because there's a little one above it, like a hip-bath, and you can go from one to the other easily."

"It looks nice," said Violet. "I'll just put my…"

But as she spoke, someone started shouting her name, which echoed up the river.

"If that's Terence mucking things up again, I'll brain him!" said Violet, setting off to restore peace.

Ellen slipped out of her jeans and sweater and

75

into the water, congratulating herself on the fact that she had put her costume on before coming out. It was much easier to change at home, and she was hot and tired after the long walk from Ballaghbeg.

She lay in the hip-bath pool, looking over the rocks to the sea. There seemed to be nothing in the world but sea, no end to it, unless you swam to the very edge and fell off.

"I bet the earth is flat!" she said to herself.

But she was really putting off thinking about what had happened to her.

What *has* happened to me? she thought.

It was all bound up with the back house, everything that had happened to her. "But nothing much has happened," she reminded herself. There was the girl she had seen in the mirror, where she should have seen her own reflection, and the old man at the door, and the sky seen from a window that looked out on the back of Bon Vista … the same sort of thing as Mr Carncross seeing trains, when the railway line had been submerged by neat lawns and plastic gnomes. If he could see trains where there were bungalows, she could see the sky where there was a brick wall.

And there was the mystery of the tears.

The girl she had seen reflected in the mirror had been crying.

"But the tears were on my cheek!"

I'm being haunted, she thought.

It was the first time she had actually thought it.

"People aren't haunted, only places."

"Maybe the back house is haunted."

But the back house was small, welcoming, a happy house with a happy feel to it ... and a window where things could be seen that *couldn't* be seen, a pen that wanted to say what its name was, a mirror that showed the wrong reflection, and a rusty duelling pistol hidden up the chimney.

Then she thought: I must be going mad!

She lay back in the water.

The old man... "I wonder if he was the girl's father?" she thought out loud.

"I wonder what my father was like?"

She had seen photographs, but she could not remember him, not as he had really been.

"I wonder if that girl lost her father ... if that was what made her cry?"

"I wonder if Bella can really remember him?"

"I wonder what it is like, having a father?"

"I wonder..." but she was tired of wondering, and she clambered out of the hip-bath pool and into the Blue Pool with a tremendous splashing. The mountain water was colder than the sea, but more refreshing. She lay on her back and floated.

Just for a moment she was Ellie Bailey, Australian back-stroke gold medallist, and then Violet appeared over the rocks.

"Terence has disappeared," she said.

Ellen didn't think that that was any loss.

"We'll have to look for him," said Violet. "He has no sense at all."

"All right," said Ellen, and she clambered out of the pool, and swiftly changed her clothes.

They came down the bank of the river past the tent where Douglas and Thomas were happily building a stone dam and, having handed down a firm injunction that they were not to leave the spot, the two girls set off to hunt the missing Terence.

"I bet he's at the Leap," said Violet.

"He'd better not be," said Ellen. "It's dangerous."

"Is it?"

"That's how it got its name, people drowning," said Ellen.

"I thought it was called Peadar's Leap," said Violet. "Doesn't that mean somebody jumped it?"

"Jumped off it," said Ellen. "Not over it. He was some sort of rebel or something, it might have been in the Ninety-Eight, and they had him cornered on the cliffs. He realized that he wasn't going to escape, and he was determined that he wasn't going to be taken alive. So he jumped off the cliffs instead, and he was drowned."

"That's a *lovely* story," said Violet. "I do like a happy ending."

"It gets worse," said Ellen, with relish. "He had been going to marry a girl from the town, and when he jumped in she went mad with grief like Ophelia. She kept coming out here to sit on the rocks and look down into the water, and one day they found her wrap here, and nothing else. She'd taken a bellyflopper after him!"

"That's nice!" said Violet.

They had come to the rope bridge. Gingerly Violet looked down. The waves rushed up the narrow channel to disappear into the cliff face, with a low throaty gurgle. On a low ledge, just by the split in the rocks, was Terence.

"Terence!" Violet called.

He didn't hear her. "*Deliberately*!" said Violet.

"I don't think I like your little brother," Ellen said, as they started down the narrow goat-path to the foot of the Leap.

"He couldn't get in there, could he?" said Violet, indicating the narrow chasm in the rock.

"I wonder... No, I don't think so," said Ellen.

A wave broke against the ledge on which Terence was sitting, and flowed back again, white and frothy. There was a sucking, roaring noise as its wash continued up the narrow slit in the rock.

"Were you looking for me?" Terence asked innocently, as they stood by the guard-rail, just above his head. "That rail is to stop kids getting down here," he explained. Then he added, "and girls."

There was a rumble and a rush of water came back out of the narrow cave. "It's very dark," said Violet, leaning against the rail to look up the cave. "The roof gets lower and lower, but the darkness goes on for ever. I wish I had a torch."

"We could get one," said Terence. "We could rope ourselves together and…"

"No!" said Violet.

"I wonder if we *could*," said Ellen, hesitantly. "I wonder if…"

"No!" said Violet. "You come up out of there, Terence. I'm not risking my neck for you."

At that moment a large wave broke against the ledge on which Terence sat, drenching him.

"Wait'll I get you home!" said Violet. "Come on up!"

"If you insist," said Terence. "Girls!"

They frog-marched him up the steps, but going up was much worse than coming down.

"Did you see this?" said Terence, pointing out the verse cut in the granite rock.

Violet read it out:

O come to me, beloved,
And stay here by my side.
O come to me, beloved,
At the turning of the tide.

I'll come to you, beloved,
I'll stay by your side.
I'll come to you, beloved,
At the turning of the tide.

"It's supposed to be a conversation between them," explained Ellen. "His ghost says the first bit, and she says the second … after that, splash!"

"Did she jump in?" said Terence. "I bet she was drowned!"

"What a lovely little boy!" said Ellen.

"I'm not a little boy," said Terence. "And I wouldn't drown. It's not as deep as all that, really. It looks much worse than it is, because the water churns about between the rocks. I bet I could…"

"Shut up, Terence!" said both girls.

"I'll belt you one if you don't," said Violet, who had lost all patience with her brother.

"You couldn't!" he said.

"I'll get Paul to belt you one then," said Violet.

The tenters having been collected, it was a frosty party that made its way back to Bon Vista. Terence disappeared again as they came to the harbour, but this time no one chased him.

"He's getting far too big for his boots," said Violet. "I hope he falls in somewhere and gets soaked."

They went down on to the sand, and strolled along, leaving the tenters to follow the road.

"I think I'm being haunted," said Ellen.

"Are you?" said Violet, adding quickly: "I don't see how you can be. I don't believe in ghosts, but what's it like?"

Ellen thought about it. "Not frightening," she said. "Interesting."

Violet gave a mock shudder. "Tell me," she said.

So Ellen told her.

"And the pen just writes, without you doing it?" Violet asked.

"It is called automatic writing," Ellen said. "I looked it up in one of Father's books. It happens to a lot of people, only they usually turn out to be haunted by Mozart, and write symphonies."

"Who is haunting you?"

"I don't know," said Ellen. "But ... well, I think it might be that girl."

"What girl? The one you saw in the mirror?"

"Yes. I was looking at myself in the mirror,

and suddenly I saw her instead, and she was crying, and then she faded away, and there was a tear on my cheek ... it's as if I looked like her for a moment, only that couldn't be, because she was very beautiful."

"I see what you mean," said Violet. "I mean, you aren't very beautiful, are you?"

Ellen didn't answer. "Sorry," said Violet.

"Well, I'm not beautiful," said Ellen. "But I wasn't thinking about that. I was thinking about the girl. I think she was a young girl in the back house once, just like me, and that's why I'm seeing her, and she's trying to talk to me ... make me write what she wants to say, I mean, not talk. Ghosts don't talk."

"What does your mother say about it?"

"I haven't told her. I haven't even told Bella everything ... you're the first person."

"Oh," said Violet.

"I suppose I don't want to tell them," said Ellen. "I would if I was afraid, but I'm not. I don't think either of my ghosts would do me any harm. And ... I don't know ... it feels like a personal thing, absolutely for me."

"I'd like to see one of your ghosts," said Violet, who was getting a little suspicious. Ghosts that no one else could see would be very easy to make up. "I don't think I've ever seen a ghost," she added.

"You don't know that," said Ellen. "You might have seen one, and not known what it was. I didn't know the old man was a ghost … I thought he was a … some sort of mirage, I suppose."

"Hmmph!" said Violet, sceptically.

They walked on. Ellen was silent. It was all very well for someone who didn't believe in ghosts to talk about how nice it would be to see one … but Ellen had decided that she did believe in ghosts.

I wish I could prove it, she thought. I wonder if there's any way I could…

"I bet I don't see one," said Violet. "I bet I…"

CHAPTER 8

The Mooneys sat around the dining-room table in Bon Vista.

Mr Mooney was at the top of the table.

On his left-hand side sat Paul, Terence, James, Douglas and Thomas.

Mrs Mooney sat at the bottom of the table, beside the teapot, with the Baby Mooney close at hand, where she could get at it if it yelled.

On her left sat Mary, Violet, Sally, Anna and Harold. Harold wasn't a girl with a funny name, he was just one boy too many for the other side of the table.

All the Mooneys were looking at their sausages.

"They got a bit burned, I'm afraid," gulped Ellen.

"Never mind," said Violet. "Mine is delicious!" and she took a brave bite from the charred morsel on the plate before her.

Ellen had been reading the problems page in one of her mother's magazines. She had just got to Heartcrossed (Bristol) when the doorbell went. She went out, answered it, and came back to find dark smoke coming from the cooker.

"Would you like some bread?" Ellen asked.

"I want chips!" said Terence.

"Shut up, Terence!" said Mrs Mooney, Mary and Violet, together.

Ellen retreated to the kitchen.

"There's a burning smell in here," said Mrs Bailey, who had been out in the vegetable garden.

"Ellen had a slight accident," said Bella.

"It would be Ellen!" said Mrs Bailey, straightening the little pink hat she wore.

Bella looked at the pink hat. She opened her mouth to say something, and stopped.

When Ellen collected the plates from the dining-room, most of them were complete with the remnants of blackened sausage.

Very quickly she got them into a newspaper and into the bin, out of her mother's way.

She heard her mother talking in the hallway.

"I hope the children enjoyed their teas," said Mrs Bailey. "They'll need a good meal, if they're going to the fireworks."

Ellen waited for the reply.

"Tea was delightful," said Mary Mooney, carefully. The eldest Mooney immediately went up several places in Ellen's estimation.

"Mine was ouch!" said Terence. "I was only going to say that ... yow! Stop it!"

"Violet!" exclaimed Mrs Mooney. "Mary! What are you doing to Terence?"

"Pulling his ears," said Violet.

"Well, don't!" said Mrs Mooney. "I don't know what Mrs Bailey will think of you."

"I like pulling his ears," said Violet.

But the conversation moved on from sausages, without Terence managing to tell his version. Ellen decided that she was indebted to Violet and Mary, who had intervened decisively on her behalf, and to the other Mooneys who had borne the meal in silence.

"You're lucky they didn't tell on you," said Bella. "I would have."

"Oh yes," said Ellen. "You'd have enjoyed doing that, I'm sure!"

The bell rang and Bella disappeared.

Before she came back, Mrs Bailey rushed in with the eight-year-old from the back bedroom who had cut himself on a broken lemonade bottle on the beach. He had to be bathed and soothed by Ellen, and then taken to the doctor.

"God alone knows where his parents are!" exclaimed Mrs Bailey, to whom the works of her paying guests were most mysterious. "I think they might have been here, considering."

"Considering what, Mother?" asked Ellen.

"What?"

"Yes, what?"

"I don't know," said Mrs Bailey, straightening her pink hat. "Don't be silly. Get that child to the doctor at once. He might get lockjaw."

"I'll consider myself considered," said Ellen, and went, dragging a reluctant Robert Bruce Whitaker of Larne behind her.

As a result of the expedition to the doctor, Ellen was not involved in the second sitting of High Tea at Bon Vista, which was served by the proprietor in person, complete with pink hat. There were so many Mooneys that Mrs Bailey had arranged to feed them separately from the other guests, which was all very well, but meant twice as much work.

Ellen left Robert Bruce Whitaker in his parents' hands and went off to hang up her anorak.

She hung it in the closet beneath the stairs, beside her father's old tweed jacket. She paused for a moment, and felt the sleeve. The rough tweed brushed through her fingers.

"I wonder if my father was like hers?" she said to herself. The old man at the back house door had looked kind. He had reached out a hand toward her. "I wonder if he could see me?" she thought.

"But he was only a ghost."

"I wonder if my father knows about all this?"

Violet was waiting for her in the drawing-room upstairs. "Where have you been?" she asked impatiently.

Ellen told her. "And he bit me!" she said. "He didn't want to go, so he bit me. But I took him just the same."

"Show me the bite," said Violet.

There wasn't much of a bite left, only a faint red mark. "It was sore at the time," said Ellen, apologetically.

"Poor you!" said Violet. "Now lead on to the ghosts!"

They went down to the kitchen and out of the yard door, making for the back house.

"It's very pretty, isn't it?" said Violet, admiring the roses that climbed up the drain-pipe, and the rain barrel at the corner. "I like the blue door."

"I painted that," said Ellen proudly.

"It's all crooked," said Violet. "It must be very old."

Ellen explained what Mr Carncross had told them about the people in the house working on the Duvalier Estate. "At least, we think they probably did."

"You ought to be able to find out," said Violet.

"What do you mean?"

"Well, there must be an estate office somewhere," said Violet. "We could ask, couldn't we?"

We. If Bella had said it, Ellen would have been

cross. But she didn't mind when it was Violet…
Because Bella's my sister, and bossy, she told
herself.

"I suppose we could," said Ellen, opening the
door.

"It's very nice," said Violet, looking round the
room. "I love the wee white window … and
there's some sort of carving there, isn't there?"

"A bird," said Ellen. "That's on the mantelpiece.
Then if you look at the stair-post, you'll see
somebody's made a lion's head on top, and up in
my room there are flowers cut in the wood over
the door."

"What a funny little staircase!" Violet
exclaimed. "It's like the Seven Dwarfs' house in
Snow White, isn't it?"

"Except that real people lived here," said
Ellen. "Whoever they were. I wonder if the estate
office could help."

There was an estate office, just on the far
side of the swimming pool. The Duvalier
Estate Office … and of course Violet was right,
they would have records. "We might be able to
find out who they were," said Ellen.

They climbed the stairs, and ducked beneath
the beam in Ellen's doorway.

"Blue!" said Violet. "And all new paint smells!
I envy you … but I don't see any ghosts! It isn't
really a *ghosty* place."

"That's what I thought," said Ellen. She had made the room very cosy. The door and the window and the mantelpiece were startling white, and the walls a deep rich blue, to match the blue of the bedspread she had brought out from Bon Vista.

"It's dark, isn't it?" Violet said. "That's the only thing I don't like."

"This house is too close to Bon Vista," said Ellen. "I suppose when they built Bon Vista, they thought that no one would ever live out here again. This one was supposed to become an outhouse, or be knocked down. But it must have had a lovely setting once upon a time. From the back you can still see the mountains and the Lodge, and there is a lovely view from my ... well, there must have been a lovely view from my room, right across the bay."

"Is this the haunted window?" said Violet, hopefully stooping to look out of the window.

"It doesn't work that way," said Ellen.

"I didn't think it would," said Violet. "Let's try the writing."

So they put a piece of notepaper on the window-sill, and took turns at holding the pen to see if anything would happen.

Violet tried first.

T.O.T.T.E.N.H.A.M...

the pen spelled out.

"Tottenham Hotspur," translated Ellen, dryly.

"I couldn't help it," said Violet, as she saw the angry flush on Ellen's face. "I didn't mean it to write that."

"You're just making fun of me," said Ellen. "Ghosts don't spell out the names of football teams."

"Honestly, I didn't do a thing to it!" said Violet. "I let my mind go blank, like you said, and that's what I got."

"Try again," said Ellen.

This time the pen only moved slightly and made a squiggle on the page.

"I don't think it is a ghost thing," said Violet. "I mean, writing 'Tottenham Hotspur' is ridiculous, isn't it? And that squiggle isn't much use."

"I bet the Tottenham bit came out of your mind," said Ellen, and then she added: "I wouldn't be a bit surprised if the squiggle did too."

Violet was offended.

"You show me," she said. "You do better. Go on. You're the one who believes in it, after all!"

Ellen took the pen and stood by the window, concentrating on the back wall of Bon Vista, and hoping against hope that something would happen. There is nothing more embarrassing than to spend a whole afternoon talking about the ghosts in your back house, when the ghosts fail to perform to order.

She put the pen against the paper and waited.

"Any good?" said Violet.

"I think I felt a wriggle," said Ellen.

But there was no wriggle. The pen stayed where it was, poised between her fingers, and there was no mark on the paper.

"That's it, isn't it?" said Violet. "No ghosts for me, I knew there wouldn't be."

Ellen said nothing. She felt silly, and annoyed.

"Show me where you found the pistol," said Violet.

Ellen showed her where the pistol had been, although sensibly Violet wouldn't climb up the chimney. Ellen also showed her the remains of the pistol, and the silver initials.

"J.D.," said Ellen. "Mr Carncross said it was probably John Duvalier."

"What was John Duvalier doing up your chimney?" asked Violet, reasonably enough, but Ellen couldn't tell her.

They had exhausted the possibilities of the back house. Violet scouted around for a bit and found the head of a dog carved on a door handle, but no ghosts.

"We'll try again later," said Violet, who could see that Ellen was annoyed. "Come on, I tell you what! We'll go to the fireworks display in the Demesne, and you can show me where the Duvaliers used to live. Maybe we'll see the ghost of J.D.!"

The children at Bon Vista didn't all go to the fireworks display together.

Terence slipped off on his own.

Mary and James were left in charge of Sally, Douglas, Thomas and Anna ... and it wasn't until they were in the Demesne and at the Lawn Field that they discovered that the tent had come with them.

Harold, who was small, went on his father's shoulders.

Violet and Ellen made their way into the Demesne by the little gate behind the parish church, where Violet noticed yet another of the animal carvings, this time of a fox and pheasant, cut into the lintel.

"This was the Duvaliers' personal entrance," Ellen explained. "They rode to church from the Lodge in their carriages. It must all have been very grand."

"I'd like to see the Lodge," said Violet.

Paul and Bella had gone on ahead of the others. They were in the car-park beside the football ground.

"I don't think it is very likely," said Bella.

"I want to check the blue ones, if there are any," said Paul, doggedly. She waited for him by the Demesne entrance as he checked around the large park for the blue minibus.

"No luck?" said Bella.

Paul shook his head.

"I don't suppose it's still in Ballaghbeg," said Bella. "It is probably in England by now, or some garage in Belfast."

"That's what I thought," said Paul. "But now I'm beginning to wonder."

"Why?"

"Well, I'm pretty sure that it was our minibus that nearly ran you down the other day. If it was, that means somebody had let it stay in Ballaghbeg, and hadn't even bothered to change the colour."

"That sounds unlikely," said Bella.

"It is … if it was the minibus they were stealing," said Paul. "But suppose they were going to steal something else, and take it away in the bus?"

"And just dump it afterwards, you mean?"

"That's right. This is a small town, there aren't many policemen. I think it's still hidden here, waiting for … whatever they are waiting for."

"Why not steal it when it's wanted, instead of running a risk by holding on to it?"

"They might want to take out the insides, to fit in whatever they're going to fit in. They'd probably need a day or two for that, and then..."

"Guess what?" said Bella.

"Exactly," said Paul.

Bella looked at the crowd moving past them. "You said you were taking me to the fireworks," she prompted.

He grinned. "So I am!"

They set off up the hill together, into the gathering dusk.

As they came over the brow of the hill above the Lawn Field, the first firework illumination spluttered into life.

A bright golden goose pushing a golden egg moved jerkily along a wooden frame, spurting and whizzing.

Bella looked at Paul. The light played across his face and glinted on his fair hair.

I hope he likes me, she thought.

Ellen and Violet had found their way to the ruined Lodge, set on a slope at the far side of the Lawn Field from their own house. From the top of the slope they could see the roof of Bon Vista, and the distant spires of the town's churches.

"I think this must have been a lovely place to live," said Ellen. "Imagine it ... with the mountains behind you, and the field in front, sloping down to the sea."

"Let's have a closer look," said Violet, and they strolled around the old house, pausing for a moment to inspect the stables, where the roof had collapsed, and to rattle the iron door erected across the entrance porch. Then they went down the granite steps to the kitchen quarters.

"There's nothing to see here," said Ellen. "There used to be a kitchen garden, but somebody took all the plants."

They moved between the ruined buildings.

Suddenly, Violet went white.

There was a shuffling, snuffling sound coming from the old building.

"I ... I think we'd better go," said Violet, and turning quickly on her heel she dashed up the steps.

Ellen came after her grinning.

"That must be the hanged footman," she said, with a serious look on her face. "It's very bad luck to see him."

"I didn't see him," said Violet quickly. "I heard him."

"He looked absolutely awful," said Ellen. "Blood all over him, and his head on a silver salver, and in his hands the keys to the Master's cellar, jiggling and..."

Violet looked at her.

"Pigs," said Ellen, breaking into a grin.

Violet looked hurt. "I don't think that that

was very nice of you," she said. "I thought it was ghosts, for sure!"

"Billy Catchpole's pigs!" chuckled Ellen. "And you thought it was the hanged footman!"

"A hanged footman would have his head on his shoulders, so it wasn't even a cleverly worked out joke."

"I know I…" began Ellen, then she stopped. "What's that?" she said.

"What?"

"There's someone coming."

"So?"

"Stand still!" Ellen hissed.

They both stood very still. Someone was coming, walking very softly through the laurels.

"I don't see…"

"Shssh! I want to know what they're doing," said Ellen. "Nobody has any business being up here in the middle of the fireworks."

"*We*'re up here," Violet pointed out.

The beam of a torch flickered over the back wall of the house.

"I wonder what he's up to?" muttered Ellen, but the purr of an engine interrupted her. Suddenly there was the sound of branches breaking, and part of the laurel bush behind them began to move. A dark shape lurched out of the bushes.

"It's a lorry, or something," Violet whispered. "Hidden in the bushes."

"It isn't," said Ellen, as the vehicle lurched down on to the path beside them, and turned up toward the ruin. "It's a minibus!"

"Our minibus...!" exclaimed Violet.

"Kids!" said a voice just behind them, and they found themselves caught in the glare of a torch-beam. A man appeared, walking toward them. "What are you doing here?" he demanded.

"Why shouldn't we be here?" said Ellen.

"Trespassers!" he said. "That's what you are. This is private property. You clear off."

Ellen stood very still. Should she...?

"We're going," she said.

They turned down the embankment between the trees. The torch-beam followed them for a short distance, then flicked off.

"Down!" commanded Ellen, and they both flopped down in the long grass.

"What are we going to do?" asked Violet.

"You're going to get help," said Ellen. "I'm going back!"

"But you can't..."

"I can," Ellen said, and the next moment she was worming her way through the grass, up the slope to the Lodge.

A torchlight flickered, showing the minibus. It had moved round to the courtyard. Ellen set off diagonally up the slope. She was very puzzled.

Why should anyone hide a minibus in the Demesne ... and a stolen minibus at that.

In the distance two battleships made from fireworks were firing rockets at each other, until one of them spluttered and very realistically sank. Then a rocket split the sky, and soared high above the Lodge.

For a moment, and just for a moment, the scene was illuminated.

The minibus sat in the courtyard, and someone had let down a ramp at the back.

There was a snuffling, squealing noise, coming closer.

Ellen froze, with her face to the ground.

I wonder... she thought.

She looked up, straining to see over the top of the grass slope.

Look where wondering has got me this time! she thought.

The snuffling, squealing noise grew louder, until there was no mistaking what it was, and what was happening.

"They're stealing Billy Catchpole's pigs!"

She crawled to the edge of the grass path, and then scrambled across the path, to the shade of the narrow stone porch. Overhead a rocket burst, colouring her scarlet.

She ducked at once.

That would never do.

Do ... what was she going to do?

Let down the tyres, perhaps ... or make a lot of noise ... it didn't sound very likely.

She peered out of the porch.

There were two men, the one with the torch and another, who must have been driving the minibus. They were driving Billy Catchpole's pigs up the ramp with ash wands.

The men worked on quickly and efficiently, with only an occasional pig squeal or a muffled curse, sounds that were completely lost in the whizz and bang of the fireworks, and the distant "Oohs" and "Ahhs" of the audience.

"That's the lot, Jackie," said the man with the torch. "Catchpole will never know what's hit him!"

"Right, Arthur," said the other man.

"Ellen!" Paul hissed. "What are you..."

"They've got your minibus," said Ellen.

"Violet told us..."

"And they're filling it with Billy's pigs!"

"Not for long they're not," said Paul angrily.

He went to stand up, but Ellen grabbed him and kept him down.

"Let go of me!" Paul said.

"No Paul, you can't."

"Yes I can! I'm not going to stay here and let them get away with it."

"You *can't* tackle them, Paul!" Ellen said.

"They might have guns or something. You might get killed."

"I don't care…" Paul began.

"I do," Ellen said. "*And Bella does*."

"But…"

"We only need hold them up for a minute or two!" Ellen said, thinking rapidly. "Violet will be back with lots of people. They can stop it … *you* can't!"

The men were climbing into the minibus. In a moment they would be gone, taking the precious bus and Catchpole's pigs with them.

"I wish the police would come!" Ellen muttered.

"That's it!" burst out Paul. "*We'll* be the police!"

"We don't exactly *look* like the police, stupid," hissed Ellen.

"Don't have to," said Paul.

"STOP! THIS IS THE POLICE! WE HAVE YOU SURROUNDED!" Paul's voice rang out in the darkness. Jackie and Arthur froze.

"STAY RIGHT WHERE YOU ARE, AND THERE'LL BE NO TROUBLE!" Paul called.

"Get out of here!" Jackie said, leaping for the door of the minibus.

"DON'T MOVE! STAY RIGHT WHERE YOU ARE!"

"Try 'hands up!'" Ellen suggested.

"RAISE YOUR HANDS IN THE AIR AND

STAY RIGHT WHERE YOU ARE!" Paul called.

Uncertainly, Arthur raised his hands in the air. But Jackie was already in the minibus, trying to start the engine.

"Get in!" he yelled at Arthur.

"It's the cops, Jackie!" Arthur said.

Then a whole lot of things happened at once.

First a police car came roaring out of the night, sirens going and lights blazing. Jackie started the engine, and roared off, skidding round and bashing into the side of the police car, almost ripping the side away from it. Jackie headed for the gateway, where someone else was spotlighted in the headlights... Terence! He was clutching Thomas's tent hammer. He tried to pull the gate closed, but it was stuck fast through rust and age.

Terence raised his arm and then, it seemed to Ellen almost in slow motion, the hammer left his hand and arched towards the minibus, crashing through the windscreen. The minibus swerved, righted itself, skidded and crashed into the door of the derelict gatehouse, spilling Jackie out on his back.

There was a tremendous bang, and silence. Petrol dripped on the ground from the front of the bus, and the pigs were squealing. Suddenly people seemed to be coming from any direction.

"Are you all right?" asked Bella, catching hold of Ellen.

"I suppose so!" said Ellen. "It was Terence. He must be mad!"

"You're all mad!" said Bella. "What a silly thing to do. As if you could tackle pig stealers all by yourselves. You could all have been killed! You do keep poking your nose in where any sensible person…"

"We *didn't*," said Paul. "And don't scold Ellen. It was her idea to hold them up until the police came. If it hadn't been for Ellen they would have got clean away!"

"You were great, too!" said Ellen, still upset and shivering with fear, because Terence could have been killed, and she would have been … kind of … responsible.

"He's a little hero!" exclaimed someone else.

"I didn't do anything!" said Paul modestly.

"Not *you*!" said the someone. "The little kid. Brave kid! And such a nipper! But he knew what to do!"

A lot of people were grouped around Terence's small figure, and he showed off the small cut on his forehead.

"He did exactly the *wrong* thing!" muttered Ellen. "Nearly getting himself killed for a few pigs and an old bus!"

"We'll never hear the end of this!" groaned Paul.

CHAPTER 9

Terence was the hero of the hour. Not for the first time, Bon Vista was bursting at the seams. At first it was the police, and the doctor to put a stitch in the cut in Terence's forehead, where the flying glass from the broken windscreen had struck him.

"It almost put out my eye," said Terence. "I was lucky!"

"Plucky!" said someone, and Terence smiled modestly.

There was a telephone call from the BBC, and reporters began to arrive.

It was a situation that quickly lost its charm, from the Baileys' point of view. Ellen and Bella were kept running backwards and forwards to deal with the newcomers, and every time they showed someone up to the drawing-room where Terence held court, they were faced with the shiny face and bandaged head of "our brave little lad" as the lady from the *Ballaghbeg Observer* insisted on calling him.

"Honestly, you'd think no one else had anything to do with it!" said Mary Mooney. "After all, Violet raised the alarm, and Paul and Ellen held them up until the police arrived, and Thomas and Douglas lost a good tent hammer and our minibus is damaged beyond repair, which means no holidays in it for us!"

"I suppose it was brave of him, Mary," said Bella. "He could have been run over."

"Not Terence!" said Mary. "Everything he does works out all right for Terence, and the rest of us catch the trouble that comes after it."

Paul kept silent. He had his own views about small boys who managed to convey to grown-ups that they had done everything single-handed, and that they hadn't *really* lost a lot of blood, at the same time making sure that they were the centre of attention.

"I'm beginning to wonder if we were there at all!" Ellen grumbled.

"He's going to be insufferable," said Violet, with deep misgivings.

"Doesn't anybody like Terence?" asked Bella.

"He's awful!" said Mary. "You just don't know what it is like if you haven't lived with him. I wouldn't mind if it had been anyone else in the family, but Terence…"

"You have to see him in action to know what we mean," said Violet.

The consensus of the meeting was gloomy. The Baileys listened as the Mooneys told Tales of Terence in Terrible Technicolour. There was the time Terence ran away with the circus, actually getting as far as Dundalk, there was the time Terence told the policeman that...

"Maybe he does it because none of you like him," suggested Ellen.

"Hmmph!" said Mary Mooney.

"Double Hmmph!" said Paul.

Ellen heaved herself up out of the armchair she was sitting in, and spoke to Bella. "Would you mind very much if I left you to it? I've got a splitting head, and I'd like to get to bed."

"I'll consider myself put-upon," said Bella, making a face, for there was a mountain of dishes.

"You do look tired," Mary said to Ellen. "You should go straight off to bed."

"I'll help Bella with the dishes," Paul volunteered.

Violet looked at Mary, and Mary shrugged. "I wonder what makes the dishes so *specially* attractive tonight," Mary said. "You never offer to help *us*."

"That's because we're his sisters," said Violet. And Bella blushed.

Ellen went out to the back house.

Her head hurt, but she felt well inside. It had been an exciting day. She opened the door of the back house, and started up the stairs, running her fingers against the wall to guide herself. There was no electric light in the back house, it was candles or nothing, and the candle was beside her bed upstairs.

Paul was right about the iron bed, it was too old. The spring sagged in the middle, so that it felt like sleeping in a hammock. It should have been sent to the dustbins long ago ... not that you could put a bed in a dustbin. But sagging spring or no sagging spring she was glad to sink into the bed, pulling the clothes up around her.

An exciting day ... too much was happening. She felt as if her whole life was out of breath. She felt tired, very tired. She cuddled up, with her knees pulled up and her head bent, and closed her eyes.

She lay there for ... well, she had no idea how long.

Old houses are peculiar at night, they make noises. This one was no different from any other. As she lay in the darkness of the upstairs room she heard noises that could have been a footstep on the stair, a poker in the grate, the clearing of a throat, the rasp of a knife cutting wood. She heard all these noises, and another.

It was a rhythmic ticking noise.

Could it be the wind blowing the rose against the window?

There was no wind. It had been calm when she came across the garden, finding her way through the long grass. The tops of the trees had been still against the sky.

Ellen opened her eyes.

I ought to be afraid, she thought, but she wasn't.

She lay in the darkness and listened to the ticking sound.

"I must find out what it is!" she said to herself. She sat up in bed and felt in the orange-box for her matches. She lit one, and found the candle.

The light from the candle cast an unsteady glow, first of all picking out her fingers as she guarded it from the draught, and then casting her shadow against the wall as she stood up.

She stepped out of bed and went across to the door. She opened it, and stepped out on to the tiny landing between the two bedrooms.

The ticking came from the clock on the wall.

The clock ... going!

Ellen stood very still, her mind in a whirl.

A light shone up the stairs ... a soft glowing light ... the light of an oil-lamp.

Half of her wanted to go back into her bedroom, jump into bed, and pull the bedclothes over her head ... the other half *wondered*, and the wondering won.

She moved softly down the stairs.

There was a fire in the hearth, glowing pleasantly. A fat black pot hung over it.

A tall woman was tending the pot. She turned from it with a ladle in her hand, and said something to the white-haired man who was sitting by the fire, paring the figure of a wooden doll with a short-bladed knife.

It was the old man from the garden.

He looked up.

He must see me, Ellen thought.

The old man smiled at her.

It was a *loving* smile, and Ellen felt the loving go through her. He beckoned to her to come down the stairs, he…

…and then the room seemed to shiver … and Ellen found herself standing on the bare boards of the staircase in the candlelight.

She stood very still, and closed her eyes. She felt warm, comfortable, *wanted*.

Somehow she found her way back to her bedroom. She got into bed, but she could not sleep.

A little later, she heard footsteps on the stairs.

"Who is that?"

"Me … Bella."

"Come in a minute, will you … please?"

"I'm exhausted," Bella grumbled. "All those dishes. Oh, and Mother's made a mistake with her hair-rinse, and her hair is blue … that's why she's wearing the hat in the house…" Her voice

110

faded away as she came into the room. "Ellen! What's the matter?" she said, anxiously.

"I think I've seen a ghost."

"*What*?"

Ellen told her, in as much detail as she could remember.

"And it wasn't like, well … ghosts … at all. It was as if I'd come into a room with a real family in it … real people … and it was as if I was one of them, and they were expecting me, and wanting me to be there. They *belonged* here … the woman was cooking and the man was carving a wooden doll … I suppose that that's why there are so many carvings in the house. Oh, it was *odd* … they had old clothes on, and things like that, but they were just getting on with their lives … and it was as if I was part of their lives, a part of their family."

"You mean they saw you as well?"

"I think so," said Ellen. "No, I'm sure so."

Bella shook her head. "That couldn't be right. If they were in their time, living in this house, you couldn't be. Time would be all wrong, wouldn't it? Unless you were haunting them … and you couldn't haunt them, because you hadn't been born in their day, had you?"

Ellen looked puzzled. "I suppose…" she said, then she stopped, and thought for a bit, and her face cleared.

"The girl with the tears!" she exclaimed. "That's who they saw!"

"What girl?"

Quickly, Ellen told her. "And don't you see, that's what happened. I don't exist in their world, because I haven't been born yet. But she does, and she lived here, with them ... her father and mother. And now, for some reason I don't understand, she is showing me what she saw ... showing us this house in the past, and how happy her family was ... it's as if she was showing off holiday snaps, except that these aren't photographs ... she's showing me real people."

"Sounds fantastic to me," said Bella. "Are you sure you aren't making it all up?"

Ellen didn't answer.

She was thinking.

"The business with the pen," she said. "I'm sure that that's the same thing, only she can't manage it properly so she's showing me pictures instead."

"Were you scared?" asked Bella. "You don't sound as if you were."

"No," said Ellen. Then she added: "I suppose I am a bit, now, thinking about it ... but I couldn't be at the time."

"I think you're just over-excited," said Bella. "I don't think you saw anything. You're talking as if this girl was showing you a picture, two performances nightly. I'm sure ghosts aren't like that."

"I don't care what you think they're like," said Ellen. "All I know is what I saw!"

"I haven't seen anything," said Bella. "That's all I know. And I'm out here as much as you are."

They thought about it.

"I suppose there must be something about *me*," said Ellen. "I know I … well, I *felt* what the girl was feeling, didn't I? I know I did on the stairs…" she began, awkwardly, but then she couldn't find words to finish it that wouldn't sound silly. She had felt *loved*. "And there was the tear … it was on my cheek."

"Why not me?"

"Maybe you are too old, or something," said Ellen. "Why doesn't matter anyway, as far as I'm concerned. It is *happening* to me."

"Y-e-s," said Bella, doubtfully.

"Don't expect me to explain," said Ellen. "I don't know what's happening. I'm waiting to be told … that's it. And that's what we've got to do *now*."

"What?"

"Try the pen and paper again," said Ellen, scrabbling in the orange-box.

"Are you sure we should?" said Bella doubtfully.

"You said nothing ever happened to you here," said Ellen. "Now you're afraid in case something does!"

They sat together on Ellen's bed.

The pen twitched in Ellen's hand.

"Try not to think about it," Ellen said. "Anything you think may interfere with it. When Violet did it, we got Tottenham Hotspur!"

Nothing happened.

"Are you sure you're not thinking?" said Ellen, severely.

"Quite sure," said Bella.

The pen scraped a little, and moved on the page. It drew a shaky line.

"What's that?" said Bella, but Ellen's free hand came over hers in a gesture of silence.

I....C..O..U..L..D....N..O..T....T.E..L..L....T.H..E..M.

The pen jerked, and stopped.

"*I could not tell them*," Bella said. "What on earth does that..."

"Stop!" said Ellen. "I think it's happening again."

M..Y....N..A..M..E....I.S....M..A..R..G..A..R..E.T

"My name is Margaret!" exclaimed Bella. "It's marvellous! Here, let me try!"

"No!" said Ellen, but Bella had grabbed the pen.

She held it loosely over the paper.

Nothing happened.

"I don't think much of that," she said. "I think you're just doing it yourself!"

"Keep quiet," said Ellen. "I'm going to try again. You think of a question. We'll both concentrate on it, and maybe this thing will answer."

"What sort of question?"

"Something like 'What is your second name?'" said Ellen, and quickly she wrote it out on the paper, beneath the two neat lines of copperplate script.

"It writes much better than you do," said Bella.

"I can't be writing for it, then, can I?" said Ellen. The pen twitched. "I think it's coming."

M..A..R..G..A..R..E..T

wrote the pen, and stopped.

"Oh, hurry up," said Bella.

I....C..O..U....

The pen stopped and wavered for a moment, the nib scratching the paper.

I....C..O..U..L..D....N..O..T....T..E

"I could not tell them," said Bella, impatiently.
"We've already had that one!"

The pen twitched, and lay still against Ellen's
fingers.

"You spoiled it!" Ellen said.

CHAPTER 10

"It doesn't look like an office to me," said Violet. "It looks like a cottage."

But the sign in the window said McKibben & King Estate Agents, and beneath that, in gold lettering, Office of the Duvalier Estate.

"I don't think there's much left of the estate," said Ellen.

They opened the door and went inside. There was a long wooden desk painted a wine red, with a blotter on top of it, a desk calendar, and a sign saying Agent for the Binstaple Building Society.

The Agent for the Binstaple Building Society was sitting by a single-bar electric fire, reading a book.

"Good morning!" said Ellen, politely.

He didn't move a muscle at first. Then his head turned slowly, as though it was worked by strings, and equally slowly his glasses slipped down until they lodged on the tip of his nose.

Ellen and Violet smiled politely.

"Good morning!" he said, putting down his book. He seemed to draw all his muscles together and, with a great heave, he unwound his long thin body from the chair, and stood up. He wore a shabby black suit that was too small for him, and a high wing collar, yellowed with age.

"What can I do to help you young ladies?" he said.

"Are you the Agent for the Duvalier Estate?" Ellen asked.

He put his hands on the desk top, beside the blotter. They were well-kept hands, apart from the smudges of ink by the finger-tips. "What there is of it," he said.

"I think you get our ground rent," said Ellen. "So there must still be some of it."

"Death duties," said the man. "You wouldn't believe…" but his words trailed away into nothing. He straightened his glasses. "What can I do to help you … er … young ladies?" he said, as though the sentence had just occurred to him.

The glasses slipped down his nose again, and again in slow motion he pushed them back into position, so that the sides of the frames nestled on the twin white marks at the top of each nostril.

"We," said Ellen, "that is I, live in 167 Sea Parade, and I wanted to find out about it."

He looked at her over the top of his glasses.

"Why?"

It was not an unreasonable question, but unfortunately Ellen hadn't prepared an answer. "I'm trying to trace a ghost" didn't seem to be a very sensible thing to say to the local Agent for the Binstaple Building Society. Mr McKibben or Mr King, whichever one he was, would probably chase her out of the office.

"I, er…" Ellen began.

"She has to do a project for school," said Violet, with a quick glance at Ellen.

"Yes, that's right," said Ellen, hurriedly. "A project."

"On local history," said Violet.

"I have to do a project on local history," repeated Ellen, feeling foolish.

"And she's starting with her own house," said Violet.

"And she's … I mean I'm starting with my own house," said Ellen.

"Hmmm." He looked at them for a moment, seeming to consider, and then he said, "Come this way," and lifted the wooden flap at the end of the desk to let them through.

"You've come to the right place," he said, leading them slowly … so very slowly … across the well-worn lino past the electric fire to the other side of the room, where a door opened off it. He stopped at the door and fumbled for what

119

seemed an eternity with a ring full of keys. He had just found the right one when his glasses slipped down his nose. He abandoned the key, and pushed back the glasses, then the key search had to begin again.

"Ahem!" said Ellen politely.

"I think that that's it," said Violet politely, indicating a key.

He picked the one she pointed at, and sure enough when he put it in the lock, the door opened.

It was a long, low room, with a small fireplace at one end, beside which stood a green leather armchair, much the worse for wear. Against the wall there was a bunk bed, and at the foot of the bed was a wooden cupboard, with a primus set on top of it. On the wall above hung two saucepans and a frying-pan, and on a small shelf sat a single plate, a cup, and a silver knife and fork. Along the opposite wall ran three shelves, one on top of another, and the shelves were lined with thick green ledgers. Each ledger had the year or part of a year to which it referred stamped in gold letters on the spine, but they got thinner toward the door end of the bottom shelf, and stopped altogether after the date 1952. Alongside the last of the green ledgers there was a pile of thick folders, with bold numbers, running in sequence.

"Please excuse the state of my room," he said.

"Doesn't worry us!" said Ellen, and then she wondered if she'd been rude again. "It seems a very nice room," she said. "Very ... er ... compact. Do you live here?"

"My humble hearth," he said, and then he added with something which might or might not have been irony, "Courtesy of Messrs McKibben and King!"

"I thought you were them," said Ellen. "Or one of them, anyway."

"I have not that honour," he said, and his glasses slipped down his nose.

"You should tie them on," said Violet. "Mother does."

"How astute of Mother," said the old man, and he turned from them and shambled out of the room.

Ellen looked at the line of ledgers. "Do you suppose it's all right for us to look at them?" she said. "He didn't say..."

"We won't learn anything from looking at the backs," said Violet, decisively. "Where do we start?"

"Let's find our house first," said Ellen, taking down the ledger for 1952.

It wasn't difficult to find the entry for 167 Sea Parade.

"*Premises at 167 Sea Parade, including plot*

of land and sundry outbuildings. Received John Jacobs Esq., £26."

"That doesn't tell us anything about the back house," said Violet. "I suppose it counts as 'sundry outbuildings'."

"Have you ever looked at the stairs in our house?" asked Ellen. "Right at the bottom, on the newelpost?"

Violet shook her head.

"The date is on the post. 1898. That's when it was built, and the rest of the terrace went up at about the same time. So if we can find a ledger dated before 1898 we ought to find who lived in the back house."

It was easy enough to find a suitable ledger, but when they looked up the volume for the spring of 1890, there was no Sea Parade.

"Try Winter of 1889," suggested Violet.

But again they drew a blank.

"It must have had another name," said Violet. "I know your houses were called Sea Parade, but the back houses were probably in as Labourers' Cottages, or something like that."

Ellen shook her head. "I think our back house was a bit grander than that," she said. "It was two-storey, after all, and solidly built with stone."

"A craftsman of some sort?"

"I'm going to ask *him* to help us," said Ellen.

122

"Are you sure we should?" asked Violet. "He works here. Mr McKibben or Mr King or whoever it is mightn't like him helping us. And you are supposed to be doing a project, you know, and that means finding things out for yourself."

"Well, I can't," said Ellen. "The back house doesn't seem to be here."

"All right," said Violet. "Ask him." Then she added, "Hasn't he got a funny hee-haw voice? You'd think he'd swallowed a plum!"

"I wonder if you could possibly help us a little, please?" asked Ellen, standing in the doorway.

"Certainly," he said.

He shuffled away from the fire, very very slowly.

"We can trace our house back to 1898 when it was built, but not before that."

The old man looked puzzled. "There wouldn't be an entry *before* it was built, would there?" he said.

"She doesn't mean that," said Violet, taking over. "She means, what about the old house at the back?"

"That would be an estate house," he said. "You won't find that one on the ledgers."

"Oh," said Ellen.

"Is there any way we can find out who lived there?" Violet asked.

"Yes," said the old man, with a dry grin. He moved slowly across the room and sank down on the edge of the bed. "Yes, there is. You could ask me."

Ellen looked at Violet, and then she looked back at the old man.

"I can certainly help you with that one," he said. "It would be an odd box of tricks if I couldn't!"

"Is there something ... well, special about it?" asked Ellen, *sure* that there was.

The old man pursed his lips. "Special? You could say so ... I well remember when I thought it was very special ... it's the sort of story that would appeal to a boy ... secret get-aways, and murder!"

"Murder!" said Ellen.

"Aye, murder," said the old man. "Murder most foul, according to the legend. But I wonder ... I sometimes think it might have been an accident ... or well deserved. The victim was ... well, he was a Duvalier of the worst sort, though I say it myself ... perhaps he only got what was coming to him."

He paused for a moment. "Yes, he probably deserved all he got. The Duvaliers weren't always liked here. It's one thing being the family at the Lodge, and another being liked for it."

"But what *happened*?" said Violet impatiently.

"Oh well now, that's a story. There was a man named McShane … you may have heard of him?"

"Peadar McShane?" said Violet.

"That's right."

"He was one of the United Irishmen in the 1798 rebellion against the English, wasn't he?" said Ellen. "I always thought…"

"Peadar … a rebel? Not him. He was a brave man by all accounts, but maybe with a brave man's temper as well. He was land agent to Sir John Duvalier … as hard a man as you'd meet in a day's journey, by all accounts. Sir John had his agent to the Lodge one day, to sort out some bother there was between them. The story goes that Sir John was in the library, polishing his duelling pistols, when McShane came to him. Straight away they were arguing, and Sir John lost his head, and turned one of the pistols on McShane. Well, there was a fight, and the agent bested his master. Someone heard the shot, and ran to the library … but the french window was banging in the wind, and McShane was gone. Sir John lay dead on the floor, shot by his own pistol."

"But what's this got to do with our back house?" asked Ellen, puzzled.

"McConnell's house," said the old man. "They say that that is where he fled to … for there was a young girl there, who loved him. But surely you know the story – 'I'll come to you, beloved, at the turning of the tide'?"

"Yes," said Ellen. "I know it."

"Well, legend has it that the McConnells hid Peadar McShane in that house, while the whole country was in an uproar looking for him. Then one night he slipped away, and was cornered on the cliffs … and you know the rest."

The two girls were silent for a moment, thinking.

"Even McConnell himself put down his wood knife and joined the hunt … or pretended to. The girl took him in and hid him, and the father played a double game, pretending to be the faithful retainer."

"He didn't," said Ellen angrily. "He wouldn't … he…"

"What do you mean?" said the old man. "How do you know what he might do?"

"I … well…" Ellen couldn't think of any way she could explain it. "I don't think he was like that."

The old man shrugged and rose to his feet. "Well, that's all I know about your back house," he said. He stopped and stood where he was. "I've told you all I know. Can you say the same thing?"

"What do you mean?" asked Ellen.

"I think you know something you're not telling me."

Ellen didn't know what to say. She did know something, inside herself, but she couldn't start talking about ghosts to a total stranger.

"Well?" he said.

She decided what she was going to do. "I found something," she said. "A pistol ... a bit of a pistol. It had silver initials on the butt. I think it might be one of the duelling pistols you've been talking about."

The old man raised an eyebrow, then he turned aside, and opened a case beneath the bed. He knelt there fumbling for a moment, then pulled forth an object wrapped in a faded green cloth, which he pushed aside.

A gleaming flintlock pistol, with the initials J.D. on the butt.

"The other one?" he said.

Ellen nodded.

"Where did you find it?"

"In the back house ... up the chimney."

"Well, that proves it, doesn't it? McShane hid there after he fled from the Lodge. Not that it matters now ... but McConnell must have known."

Ellen stayed quiet. She was certain the old man had not known.

It was Violet who spoke.

"Why are you here?" she said.

"Why am I working as an office boy?" he said. "That's a long story, and not a very pleasant one.

"I don't understand," said Ellen.

"Don't be so dense!" said Violet. "Don't you see? Don't you know who he is?" She turned to the old man again. "I know who you are. You're John Duvalier, aren't you? And the man McShane killed was one of your ancestors!"

They only just managed to get back to Bon Vista in time for dinner, which meant that Ellen was in everyone's bad books.

"You're too dreamy by half, my girl," scolded Mrs Bailey, but it came off Ellen like water off a duck's back. She kept trying to get Bella alone to tell her sister what had happened, but it wasn't easy.

"We found John Duvalier," she said.

Bella looked blank.

"Sir John Duvalier, his family used to live in the Lodge, and own all this land," Ellen explained, impatiently.

"Wherever is the mustard?" asked Mrs Bailey. "It isn't good enough, Ellen. You must try ... there, Bella, take that into the front room, will you, dear?"

"I'll be back," breathed Bella. "Don't go away!"

"I don't know what is going on in this house today," said Mrs Bailey. "Every time I go into a room, people are having conferences."

"Oh," said Ellen, innocently.

"That boy Terence says he's going treasure-hunting next! He told the Belshaws and, do you know, I think they believed him. You haven't been encouraging him, have you?

Ellen shook her head.

"Heavens, the oil man!" Mrs Bailey exclaimed, and she disappeared through the back door, her pink hat set firmly on her blue hair.

Bella came back into the room. "Tell all!" she ordered

And Ellen did.

"And this old man is *the* Sir John Duvalier, who owns the Lodge?" Bella asked.

"Used to … he hasn't got two pennies to rub together now," said Ellen.

"And someone from our back house killed his great-great-grandfather?"

"Not from our back house," said Ellen. "He hid there afterwards, though. It was his sweetheart who lived in our back house."

"And he showed you the pistol?"

"Yes … just like our one, only kept clean and shiny, if you know what I mean, so that it doesn't look like ours at all. He says that it proves

129

McShane hid in the back house after the murder."

"I'm not sure that I want our pistol now, if someone was murdered with it," said Bella. "Shouldn't we give it to him?"

"He doesn't want it," said Ellen. "And anyway, it wasn't murder. It was an accident. And afterwards they hunted Peadar McShane down, hounded him to death ... and Margaret tried to help him."

Bella disappeared and returned under a pile of dishes. She deposited them by the sink, and threw herself down on the sofa.

"Peadar McShane hid in our back house," said Ellen. "And Margaret ... I bet that she's the girl, you *know* ... Margaret stayed with him, while her father went out to hunt him with the others. That is what Sir John says happened, anyway. But I don't think so."

"Why?"

"I just don't believe that that nice old man would lie to anybody," said Ellen. "I think Margaret hid Peadar somewhere here without telling her family. *I could not tell them.* Remember? I don't believe that her parents knew that he was hidden here. I think she had to keep it secret."

"But you don't know that, do you?" said Bella. "You just think it."

"I *feel* it," said Ellen. "Don't you see... I *know* them. I know what they were like."

The bell rang again.

"I'll go," said Ellen.

When she came back into the room she was looking serious.

"What do you think about it?" she asked Bella.

Bella shrugged. "I haven't seen anything," she said. "I don't know what to say. You think you've seen this family..."

"I have," said Ellen. "Definitely ... there's no mistake about that. I've done more than that ... I've *felt* what they were like ... at least I've felt what Margaret felt about them ... as though her father were my father..."

"Now you're being romantic," said Bella.

"Maybe I am," said Ellen. "But I know what I felt don't I?"

She felt a part of the McConnell family, as Margaret must have felt ... she had felt what Margaret had felt...

"And something went wrong," said Ellen. "And I don't know what ... but she's trying to tell me."

"Hmmph!" said Bella.

"It must be miserable for her, being a ghost," Ellen said. "I wouldn't like to be one."

"You haven't got a dark secret," said Bella,

jokingly. "It's only people with a dark secret who can't rest when they die."

"If I knew what her secret *was*..."

"Yes, well..." said Bella impatiently.

"She could rest in peace then, couldn't she? She wouldn't need to be a ghost any more!"

CHAPTER 11

The three girls sat in Ellen's bedroom. Bella and Violet were on the bed, and Ellen sat on a pile of cushions which she had brought out from Bon Vista.

They had placed a tea-chest upside down beside the bed, to act as a table. On it lay the pen, some notepaper, and the remains of the flintlock pistol.

"Who is going first?" said Violet.

Bella looked uncomfortable. "I don't know whether we should be doing this," she said. "I've been thinking about it. It's like holding a seance, isn't it?"

"I think it's exciting," said Violet.

"I don't think seances are a good thing," said Bella slowly. "I don't like the idea of disturbing people who are, well, *dead*. We don't know what we're meddling with, do we? It is like sticking a bit of bare wire into an electric socket, and hoping that it won't blow up in our faces."

"Don't be silly," said Violet. "I don't see what all the fuss is about."

"I do," said Ellen. "But I think you're wrong, Bella. This is different."

"Oh, why?"

"This time the dead are disturbed, aren't they? We know it, because one of them has *disturbed* us. Margaret started this, we didn't. We aren't meddling in something that isn't our business, we've been asked to help, and we're helping."

"Still…" said Bella.

"Look," said Ellen. "I agree with you in a way. This writing business is the sort of thing people do who want to meddle in things … a dangerous party game, most of the time. If we did that, we'd deserve anything awful that might happen to us, because we'd be putting in our noses where we weren't wanted. But this time, we know Margaret is unhappy. We know what she's unhappy about … that she couldn't tell her parents something … we know she's trying to tell us what it was. Maybe, if she can do that, it might stop her *being* a ghost. She could just fade away, or whatever ghosts do."

"So we'd be doing her a favour," said Violet. "Come on then!"

Bella still looked doubtful. "We don't know that," she said. "It's only what we think."

Ellen looked troubled. "I don't know what I

can say to convince you, except that I'm convinced. Whatever happened to Margaret and Peadar McShane, she couldn't tell her parents about. She had to keep pretending that she didn't know where he was, when all the time he was hidden in the house."

"Up the chimney!" said Violet.

"Well, maybe … though it would have been a hot seat! But that isn't what matters. What matters is that she had to deceive her parents, or betray Peadar."

They sat and thought about it.

"After he drowned, they must have found out about it," Violet said.

"But we don't know *what* she couldn't tell them, do we? We're assuming that it was something to do with Peadar McShane, but we don't know. If we're going to help her, we've got to find out what it is that has kept on troubling her all these years, so that she couldn't rest. It must be very difficult for a dead person to come back and tell us things … but she's trying very hard to do it, and that means it must be important to her."

"All right," said Bella. "I think we should go ahead."

"Good," said Ellen.

"I don't like it, though. And I'll only do it seriously … no games, agreed?"

Violet and Ellen agreed, gravely.

135

Violet took the pen.

"Ask it: 'What is your name?'" said Ellen. "It's done that before."

"It's a 'her' not an 'it', or rather she is," said Violet. "Now everybody concentrate. Ghost: What is your name?"

Nothing happened.

"Try writing it down," suggested Ellen.

What is your name? Violet printed.

When she had stopped writing, the pen hung listlessly between her fingers … then, slowly, it began to twitch.

T.O.T.T.E.N.H.A.M…

"We said no joking!" said Bella, in a warning voice. "I'm not," groaned Violet.

H.O.T.S.P.U.R

wrote the pen,
with a final flourish on the R.

"I think that's because of my brother Harold," said Violet, looking embarrassed. "He's always getting me to solve puzzles he's made up, and the answer is usually Tottenham Hotspur."

"What sort of puzzles?"

"Small person in meat with warm heels," said Violet. "Not very clever ones."

"The writing is different," pointed out Bella, who had been looking at it. "I think that that's Violet writing from her own mind, not Margaret McConnell's."

"You take the pen this time," said Violet, handing it to Ellen. "It seems to work best for you anyway."

Ellen took the pen and wrote down the question. "What is your name?"

M..A..R..G..A..R..E..T

"What is your second name?" she wrote.

M..C..C..O..N..N..E..L..L

"There!" said Ellen. "I told you it was her!"

"Is there something you want to tell us?" wrote Ellen.

M..A..R..G..A..R..E... and there was a moment's hesitation *...E..T.* The pen stopped, then jerked, then

I....D..I..D....N..O..T....D..I..E

"What does that mean?" said Bella, looking at it. "Of course she died. She wouldn't be a ghost otherwise."

"Shut up," said Ellen. "It's starting again!"
"I feel peculiar!" said Violet.

I....C..O..U..L..D....N..O..T....T..E..L..L....T..H..E..M
The pen stopped.
"What?" Ellen wrote.

M..A..R..G..A..R..E..T....M..C..C..O..N..N..E..L..L

The pen stopped abruptly and fell back against Ellen's hand.

"It's finished," said Ellen.

"I'm not sorry," said Bella, standing up. "I don't want anything more to do with it, and I don't think you should either. I vote we never try it again."

Violet nodded. "It made me feel goose-pimply."

"It was exciting," said Ellen, looking at the words on the page. "It was a peculiar feeling but … no … I wouldn't want to do it again."

"I'm off to the butcher's," said Bella. "Mother will have a fit if there's no meat."

That left Violet and Ellen alone in the upstairs room.

"I wonder what she … it … *Margaret* was trying to tell us," said Ellen, and then she read out the words on the paper.

"*Tottenham Hotspur…* I think we can forget that… *Margaret McConnell* … we know that was her name, so that's right... *Margaret* ... that's where it stopped ... e ... t *I did not die* ... but she must have, or she wouldn't be a ghost... *I could not tell them* ... well, 'them' probably means her parents... What couldn't she tell them, though? *Margaret McConnell* ... that's just her name again, and I don't see that it's any help."

"I did not die. I could not tell them," Ellen said again, musing.

"That's almost meaningless," said Violet. "We know she died."

Ellen looked thoughtful.

"Maybe she couldn't tell them that she was going to commit suicide," said Violet. "Because they'd have been upset."

"They'd have been just as upset when she did it!" said Ellen. "I don't see how telling them would have helped."

"They might have stopped her doing it."

"*If* she wanted to do it, she certainly wouldn't tell them. But I don't think that's it."

"What is it then?" said Violet wearily.

Ellen said nothing.

"You just don't know," said Violet. "I bet you don't."

"I *might* know," said Ellen. "I think I've just had an idea that might ... well, it might explain everything ... if I'm right."

139

"Well? What is it?"

"I'm not going to tell you till I know," said Ellen.

"But…"

"Don't ask me to!" said Ellen. "It isn't fair. I'll tell you tomorrow. I want to have another look at something, and I can't do that until tomorrow."

"Tomorrow is ages away," Violet objected. "*Why* tomorrow?"

"It is a question of tides," said Ellen.

CHAPTER 12

"I'm coming too," said Terence.

"No, you're not," said Violet, with equal determination.

"If it hadn't been for me…" Terence began.

"Shut up, Terence!" said Paul, Mary and Violet.

"You shouldn't say shut up to me," said Terence. "It isn't polite!"

"I'll polite you!" said Paul.

Terence put on his politest face. "Please, Violet, may I come with you?"

"No," said Violet.

"There you are," said Terence. "She still said 'no'!"

"Serve you right!" said Paul.

"I stopped the pig-stealers!" said Terence. "You saw my picture in the papers!"

"*Terence!*" He escaped with his life from the drawing-room, but only just.

Half an hour later, Violet and Ellen departed. It was a clear bright day, and the sun shone down on them, casting their shadows against the turf on the clifftop.

"I hope he doesn't follow us," said Violet.

"Terence is a terrible nuisance, even if he is your brother," said Ellen.

"Mother says he's going through a stage," said Violet. "That would be all right, if we didn't have to go through it with him!"

They started the slow descent of the Long Stair to the winding path along the rocks. It was a wild and lonely place for a walk, though the tide was at low ebb. Far below them they could see the seaweed swirl around the dark rocks.

They came to the rope bridge and crossed it. Then Ellen led the way down the goat-path to the stone with the inscription.

"I wanted to know exactly what it said," she said. "And I'm right! I just know I'm right!"

Violet read the inscription.

"O come to me, beloved,
And stay here by my side,
O come to me, beloved,
At the turning of the tide.

I'll come to you, beloved,
I'll stay by your side,
I'll come to you, beloved,
At the turning of the tide."

"I wonder who wrote it," Ellen said. "Someone with a sense of humour."

Violet looked blank.

"Perhaps it was Peadar himself," said Ellen.

"He couldn't have. He was dead!"

"I wonder if he was dead?" Ellen said, with a glance at Violet's face, to see how she was taking it.

"You…"

"I wonder if he *was* dead?" Ellen repeated. "It doesn't say anything about *that* on the stone, does it? It just asks her to come here at the turning of the tide."

"When the tide is right out, or right in," said Violet. "So what?"

"Right out," said Ellen. "It would have to be right out."

"Why?"

"I think it must be possible to get in there, when the tide is full out," said Ellen. "You remember what Terence said? He thought he could get in, and the tide was high that day."

"You mean that Peadar McShane didn't drown … he swam in there?" Violet looked at the dark slit in the rocks. "He couldn't!"

"He was a local man. He would have known the rocks well, and he knew the tides. I can't be certain, but I think there may be a short time, maybe only a matter of minutes, when the tide

143

level drops enough to allow someone to climb into the caves through that gap."

"But you said people had drowned…"

"Of course I did … but I was talking about McShane and Margaret, wasn't I? Nobody bathes here now … not that most people would want to. But the place got its reputation *because* McShane and Margaret died here."

"And you think it may not be as bad as it looks?"

"That's right," said Ellen. "Peadar McShane knew what he was doing. He couldn't go free around here, and he would have had to live a life in hiding. So he chose to let himself be seen … *and he let himself be seen to die*. Then, just to complete the picture, his sweetheart had to die too. O come to me, beloved, at the turning of the tide. And that's just what she did. She came here every day, and they thought she was mad. But she wasn't mad. And one day she didn't come back, and everyone thought she had drowned. I suppose they slipped away and…"

"You mean she didn't drown at all?"

"'I did not die'," said Ellen. "'I could not tell them.' I could not tell them *that* I did not die. If I'm right, that's what Margaret's been trying to tell us. She loved her parents, but she was running away with McShane. When she disappeared, her parents must have been in a

144

terrible state ... and she knew they *had* to be. If they hadn't been so upset, someone might have begun to wonder about the 'drowning' that never was. No, her parents had to *believe* she was dead, because they weren't the sort of people who could carry out a deception like that."

"You could be right, I suppose," said Violet.

"I think I am," said Ellen.

They fell silent.

"I wonder if we could prove it...?" said Ellen.

"How?"

"Well, if it was possible to go in there then, it should be now, shouldn't it?" said Ellen eagerly. "I ... well, I feel I sort of owe it to Margaret, in a funny way ... and..."

"You want to know," said Violet.

"It's not that I'm *just* curious," said Ellen. "It's more than that. I want *her* to know that I know, that someone understands what happened, and why she had to lie to her father and mother ... she loved her father, I know she did, and he loved her ... and then she had to do that to him ... it must have been awful, knowing he would never know what had happened, could never know, because it would have been too dangerous."

"You really care about it, don't you?" said Violet.

Ellen nodded. "I can feel it ... what she felt. I

145

don't properly remember my own father ... but I can feel what she felt ... and I want it to be put right, if I can."

"But how would it be put right...?"

"She wants someone to know," said Ellen. "Someone who will understand what she felt about her parents ... that's what she's been trying to do. And there's only one way I can know for sure, isn't there?"

There was a pause.

"I'm going in with you," said Violet.

"You don't have to..."

"I don't want to," said Violet. "I don't really understand why it matters to you, but two would be safer than one."

"You see..." Ellen started to say, but she could not explain. How could she? Violet's father was there, any time she wanted him. Violet couldn't know what it felt like ... and what it must have been like for Margaret McConnell.

"Come on," said Violet. "If we've got to, let's get it over with."

"Are you sure?" said Ellen. "I mean, I'm the one it matters to. If you..."

"Are you coming, or do I have to pull you?" said Violet, slipping under the rail and down on to the ledge where Terence had been soaked on their earlier expedition.

Ellen slipped down after her.

This time, the tide was at low ebb, and more of the ledge was exposed. They moved along it gingerly, their backs to the rock.

I've *got* to be right, Ellen thought to herself. I've just *got* to know.

They came close to the entrance to the slit in the rock. Just by the entrance, which was no more than three feet wide, the ledge on which they were standing came to a stop. Ellen leant forward, across the divide, and put one hand on the rock face opposite her. Beneath her, dark seaweed swirled back and forth across the rock.

"We must be out of our tiny minds!" Violet muttered. She had never been a particularly brave person, and now... *I wish I was safe on dry land!* she thought to herself

"Take off your shoes," said Ellen. "I wonder if we can get through that..." She had slipped off her shoes, and she prodded at the seaweed with her right foot, seeking for a foothold. The water sucked at her foot, drawing her down. She slithered, and steadied herself against the rock face, with the water around her ankles.

"Well, I'm standing on something, anyway!" she said. "Would you put your hands around my middle, just in case?"

Violet took her by the waist.

Ellen edged forward ... slipped, her body arching backwards.

"Help!" Violet said.

But Ellen had regained her balance. She was in up to the knees, but standing, three feet *inside* the narrow cavern.

"Come on..." she said.

Violet had had enough.

She stayed where she was.

"I'm sorry, Ellen. I just don't think it's safe. I'm *sure* you're right ... they *could* have come in this way ... but I don't feel like going any further to find out."

Ellen braced herself against the rock face. "I'm on a ledge, Violet. There's no danger at all. I just want to know if they *could* ... I won't go much further, honestly I won't. Just far enough to *know*..."

Ellen didn't want to let Margaret down ... it was silly, but it suddenly mattered a lot to her.

"We've *got* to stop," said Violet, in a determined voice. "I'm sorry."

Ellen flashed her torch along the wall of rock ... the cavern seem to go on for ever, with the sides coming closer and closer together.

"When the tide comes in, this fills up," said Violet. "And we know it fills up pretty quickly, because it is well below high-water mark. We don't know how long your ledge is, or whether there's any bottom at all as you get further in. We might even be moving downwards..."

"I can't go on alone," said Ellen sadly.

"I'm sorry," said Violet. "But you've got to be sensible…"

"I don't feel sensible," said Ellen.

She felt choked. She was so near to knowing, so near to being able to do what Margaret wanted, to understanding what Margaret was trying to say … and now she would never know for certain.

They started back.

When they were in the open air again they stopped to put on their shoes. The tide had already turned and low waves were running up the Leap.

"I'm sorry," Ellen said.

"What for?"

"You were being sensible. I wasn't. I was just so interested in what we'd found out."

"What we *may* have found out," said Violet.

"We'll never prove it now," said Ellen.

"It's too narrow and dark and twisty in there," said Violet. "And too often underwater! It looks drowny to me."

"But they didn't drown! That's the whole point. It *looks* horrible, but someone who knew when to go in, when the right ledges would be exposed by the low tide … I'm sure they made it."

They clambered up on to the path, and stopped by the rail.

"It would have to be life and death before I'd go in there," Violet said.

"It *was*!" Ellen said. "If he didn't go in, they would have caught him ... and he was supposed to be a murderer. He'd killed John Duvalier in a fight, and nobody was going to believe it was an accident. No ... he was dead already, the Leap was his only chance!"

"And you think that somewhere in there there's a cave above water level, where he could hide?"

"And Margaret, in the end. Both of them!"

Ellen turned towards the path ... then she stiffened. "Oh no!" she exclaimed. "Look!"

Violet followed the direction of her pointing arm.

"Terence!" she exclaimed.

He was in the mouth of the Leap, in up to his knees, groping his way along the wall.

"Terence! Stop!" Ellen cried.

He didn't hear. Or didn't choose to hear, thought Violet.

"He won't get far, not if we couldn't," said Ellen.

"But we *could* have," said Violet. "You know we could ... we pulled back, he won't. He hasn't got the brain."

"And the tide has turned," said Ellen slowly. "It will come in, and it will rise ... and rise quickly in

150

there, because the gap is so narrow. It will wash along the gap … we've got to get him out, now!"

"You go for help," said Violet. "He's my brother I'll try to get him…"

Ellen shook her head.

A wave passed them, and the swell rose about the entrance to the cave.

"It'll be above his knees by now," said Ellen. "We haven't got any time left."

They slipped over the rail and started along the ledge. The water washed up around their ankles. Down on to the hidden ledge, and it was right up to the tops of their legs.

The torch picked out the line of the walls, but no Terence.

"Maybe he's fallen in!" said Violet.

"All we can do is keep going, and hope I was right," said Ellen. "Maybe there's a bit of this cave above the high-water mark."

And maybe there isn't, she thought, all too clearly. If there wasn't, the cave would fill with water, and they would be trapped inside it.

"We can't keep going, Ellen," Violet said. "We were so stupid. One of us should have gone for help…"

"It is too late for that now," said Ellen. "We've got to go on."

"We *can't*," said Violet, and her eyes filled with tears. "Terence…"

"We can't do anything else," said Ellen slowly. "Can't you see? We rushed in here after him without thinking, and we are trapped too. The water is already too high. We can't get out. We've got to go on."

The water swirled and crashed in the narrow rock cut, coming as high as their knees.

They found a higher ledge, and for a moment they were clear of the water, then back down again, until it lapped around their waists.

"Terence!" Ellen called.

"Terence!"

"Terence," the cave echoed their words back at them, amid the thunderous noise of the water.

The water rose.

The torch went out.

They felt their way forward, foot by foot. The water was running strongly, and the roof of the cave had come down to within a foot or so of their heads. Ellen reached up and found that she could touch it. Someone was shouting. "Terence," muttered Violet.

A wave rolled down the cave. At first only the swell reached them, then the wave itself, and Ellen found herself lifted from the ledge, and washed along. She went up and up, and did not touch anything!

"Violet!" she called.

"Ellen," said a voice to her left ... or was it

to her left? She couldn't be sure.

"The roof is higher here … there may be ledges."

Another wave came and lifted Ellen. She came against a rock and grabbed at it, holding on for dear life.

"I swallowed some," said Violet's indistinct voice.

"Help!"

The cry was from above, to their right.

Ellen heaved up on the rock, in pitch darkness, moved forward and found herself up to the neck in water again, scrabbling to hold on to the seaweed as another wave drove her arms and legs against the scraping barnacles. Then something struck her, something soft.

Violet!

She grabbed her friend's arm.

"Ellen?" said a gasping voice.

"Where are you?" someone shouted.

It was Terence.

Ellen tried to pull Violet on to the rock. Another wave roared by and caught them, lifted them, and brought them clear of the water. A quick thrust and they were on a rock ledge.

A hand touched Ellen's knee. "Who is that?"

"It's me, Violet. I think he's over there somewhere."

They felt their way along the ledge. A wave

roared in, but the water came by their ankles. "We might be all right here," Violet said.

"The tide has only started coming in," said Ellen grimly.

Then they found Terence. He was standing on the ledge, gripping the rock face.

"I'm not moving," he said.

"Oh, yes, you are!" said Ellen.

"I'll drown."

"If you stay here, you will," said Ellen, and as if to make the point, a wave broke over their feet.

"Come on," said Ellen.

"I was treasure-hunting…"

"Shut up, Terence," said Violet, and for once in his life he did.

"I hope this ledge goes on," said Violet.

"If I'm right about this place, it does," said Ellen. "If I'm wrong…"

It didn't need saying. If she was wrong, they wouldn't live to know it.

"Let's hold on to each other," said Ellen, whose eyes were beginning to grow accustomed to the dark. "If we can manage that, and keep going forward, we should be all right."

They hooked arms, Ellen in front, Terence in the middle, and Violet.

"Just hands aren't enough," said Ellen. "The tide would part us."

Terence was shivering with fear … and cold.

"We're going to be all right, Terence," Violet whispered encouragingly. "Come on."

"I … can't!"

"You can!" said Violet, shoving him forward.

It was slow progress, with the waves washing around them sometimes up to their waists, once even up to their shoulders, so that Terence was lifted from the ledge, and only saved by the linked arms of the two girls. Then they came against a sheer rock face.

"It seems to stop here," said Violet. If it did, and the water kept rising…

"No, it doesn't," said Ellen.

She felt her way along the rock face, inch by inch, till suddenly it turned … they were moving upwards…

…and the water grew shallower.

And the noise began to die away.

"I think we're through," said Violet.

The water was lapping around their ankles … and then there was no water, only sand.

"Thank goodness!" said Violet, sinking down.

"We can't stay here," said Ellen. "The sea can't be more than half-way in yet. It might reach here."

So, wearily, they scrambled on, deep in the subterranean passage beneath the cliffs.

On and on … slithering and climbing over the rocks until…

"Light!" said Ellen. "Look!"

And there was light ... just a faint glimmer of it, straight ahead, above them.

They stumbled on, and the rock floor rose, carrying them up toward the light. Now they crawled, now they walked, now they climbed ... and the light became larger and larger.

"Do you think?" Violet said.

But Ellen hadn't the energy to reply.

It was a small gap, running underneath a large stone. Ellen put her arm through. She could feel the air, see the sky.

"See if Terence can make it," said Ellen. "He's smallest."

"Head first," said Violet. "If his head will go through, anything will."

Nobody laughed.

With a squeeze and a gasp, he got his shoulders down to the ground, heaved, braced himself ... another squeeze, and a wriggle ... and he was through.

"Right," said Ellen. "You're next, Violet."

Violet made it.

Last of all came Ellen.

She had not realized that she was so tired, that her muscles had given so much. She could hardly summon the strength ... she felt her nose was going to break, as the rock scraped her face ... and then she was through, into the open air.

They lay on the ground with the sky blue and clear above them, and the sunlight on their faces.

"I'm ruined altogether," said Violet, who was first to speak.

Ellen blinked in the sunlight.

There was a rushing sound, a sea sound.

The sea…

"Look, Violet!" she exclaimed, wearily. "If that doesn't beat all…?"

"What?"

"It's the Blue River," said Ellen. "We've come round a sort of circle in the darkness. We're about a hundred yards from where we started off."

Violet sat up and looked around her.

"I was right!" said Ellen, suddenly. "I knew I was right, and I was. They did escape!"

CHAPTER 13

"We've got no evidence to prove it," said Violet.

The two girls were on the beach in front of Bon Vista, keeping an eye on Thomas and Douglas, who were tenting on the beach, with a large moat around them.

"We don't need it," said Ellen. "I *know*."

"We can't tell anyone," said Violet.

They had agreed on that. Terence had come after them, and followed their example in going down into the Leap. They had been lucky, and got away with it... But neither Mrs Bailey nor Mrs Mooney was likely to look upon the escapade in a friendly light. Ellen had wondered once too often. So a white lie was arranged. Terence had fallen into the sea, and Violet and Ellen had fished him out ... and they arrived home, wet through and exhausted, and very much the worse for wear.

Bella raised an eyebrow, but no one knew anything.

"It gives me something to threaten Terence with!" said Violet. "I wish we'd found something in the cave to show they were there … that would have made all the difference."

"Not to me," said Ellen.

"Why?"

"I can *feel* it," said Ellen. "I can't explain any better than that. I've done what I was supposed to do."

Violet couldn't make head or tail of that.

"We're a bit like them, aren't we?" said Ellen.

"How do you mean?"

"'I did not die. I could not tell them,'" said Ellen. "We didn't die, and we can't tell them either!"

"There is one more thing we could try," said Violet doubtfully.

And so that night Ellen and Violet sat in the candlelight in the little room with the blue walls and watched the pen as it jerked across the paper.

M..A..R..G..A..R..E..T

The pen stopped. It moved on again.

I....S..L..E..E..P